BOUND BY THE
PRINCE'S BABY

BOUND BY THE PRINCE'S BABY

JESSICA GILMORE

MILLS & BOON

First published in Great Britain 2020
by Mills & Boon, an imprint of HarperCollins*Publishers*
1 London Bridge Street, London, SE1 9GF

Large Print edition 2020

© 2020 Jessica Gilmore

ISBN: 978-0-263-08519-8

MIX
Paper from
responsible sources
FSC® C007454

Printed and bound in Great Britain
by CPI Group (UK) Ltd, Croydon, CR0 4YY

For Dan and Abby, always.

PROLOGUE

Eight years ago

THE CAR PURRED to a stop and the driver got out, walking as stiffly as if he were on parade to the rear passenger side and opening the door. Amber Kireyev pulled her hated kilt down to her knees before she grabbed her rucksack and shimmied out of the car under his always watchful gaze.

'Thank you, Boris,' she said with a smile, but as usual there was no glimmer of a return smile, just a curt nod.

'Princess Vasilisa.'

'Amber,' she said, as she always did. 'Call me Amber.'

But Boris didn't acknowledge her words as he stood tall and imposing, waiting for her to walk through the entranceway; he wouldn't move until he had seen her go into the building and the doors close behind her.

Amber suppressed a sigh. She knew that most people would consider selling their soul to occupy an apartment in this grand Art Deco building overlooking Central Park, especially a penthouse in one of the two iconic towers, but to her the apartment was more prison than home. Hefting her backpack onto her shoulder, she walked, chin held high, up to the doors and pressed the button for admittance. The doors swung silently and ominously open and, without a backward glance at the sun-filled afternoon, she walked inside.

The opulent high-ceilinged marble and tile foyer was so familiar to her she barely noticed its glossy splendour, but she did notice the smiling man behind the concierge desk, dapper in his gilt and navy uniform.

'Miss Amber, Happy Birthday to you.'

'Thank you, Hector.'

'Do you have something nice planned to celebrate?'

Amber tried not to pull a frustrated face. Her fellow pupils at the exclusive girls' school she attended had all thrown extravagant parties for their eighteenth birthdays, renting out hotel ballrooms or heading off to their Hampton Beach homes for the weekend. Even if they had invited her Amber wouldn't have been allowed to attend, but they'd stopped asking her years ago. 'Grandmama said that we might go out for dinner, after my lessons, of course.' Not even on her eighteenth birthday could Amber skip her dancing or deportment or etiquette lessons.

'I have something for you,' Hector whispered conspiratorially and, after looking around, he pulled out a large brown envelope from under his desk and held it out to her.

Amber's heart began to beat faster as she took in the familiar postmark. 'Thank you for letting me have it sent to your house.' Her future lay in that envelope. A future far away from here, far away from her grandmother.

'London?' Hector asked and she nodded.

'The university prospectus. London is where my parents met and worked, although we lived just outside, in a little village. I always promised myself I would go back as soon as I was old enough. Applying to university is just the first step.' She slipped the envelope into her backpack. 'Thank you again.'

'I also have this for you.' With a flourish he produced a large cupcake, extravagantly iced in silver and white. 'There's no candle. The fire alarms, you know. But Maya told me to tell you to make a wish anyway.'

'Oh, Hector.' Amber hated crying but she could feel hot, heavy tears gathering in her eyes. 'This is so kind of you and Maya. Give her my love.'

'Come see us again soon; she has a new recipe she wants to teach you.' Hector cast an anxious look up at the huge clock which dominated the vestibule. 'Your grandmother will be calling down soon; you'd better go. And Amber? Happy Birthday.'

The lift—Amber refused to say elevator, clinging onto her English accent and vocabulary as stubbornly as she could—was waiting and she tapped in the code which would take her up to the penthouse, nibbling her cake as the doors slid shut and the lift started its journey.

The doors opened straight into the penthouse hallway. Usually Amber could barely put a toe onto the parquet floor before her grandmother querulously summoned her to quiz her about her day and criticise her appearance, her posture, her attitude, her ingratitude. Amber steeled herself, ready for the interrogation, the brown envelope, safely stored in her bag, a shield against every poisonous word. But today there was no summons and Amber, half a cake still clutched in her hand, managed to make it to her bedroom undisturbed, slipping her backpack onto the floor, taking out the envelope and concealing it, still unopened, at the back of her wardrobe. She'd look at it later tonight, when her grandmother was asleep.

Sitting back on her heels, Amber checked to make sure there was no hint of the envelope visible through her clothes and then clambered up, her feet sinking into the deep pile pink carpet. Her whole room was sumptuously decorated in bright pinks and cream which clashed horribly with her auburn hair and made her pale skin look even paler. But she had as little choice in the decor as she did about her schooling, wardrobe and pastimes.

Wriggling out of the hated blazer and kilt, she slipped on a simple blue dress, brushing out her plaits and tucking her mass of hair into a loose bundle before heading out to find her grandmother. The silence was so unusual that she couldn't help feeling a little apprehensive. For one moment she wondered if her grandmother had planned a birthday surprise, before pushing the ludicrous idea away. Her grandmother didn't do either birthdays or surprises.

Padding along the hallway, she peeped into the small sitting room her grandmother preferred, her curiosity piqued as she heard the low rumble of voices coming from the larger, formal sitting room her grandmother only used for entertaining. The room was light thanks to floor-to-ceiling windows with stunning views over Central Park but stuffed so full of the furniture that had been saved from Belravia during the revolution that it was impossible to find a spot not cluttered with ornate chairs or spindly tables, the walls filled with heavy portraits of scowling ancestors.

Amber hovered, torn. She hadn't been officially summoned, but surely her grandmother would expect her to come and greet whichever guest she was entertaining.

Just a few more months, she told herself. She'd graduate in a couple of months, and by the autumn she'd be in London. She just needed to apply to university and figure out how to pay for it first. She'd saved a couple of thousand dollars from her allowance but that wasn't going to cover much more than the plane ticket.

Okay. She would worry about all that later. Time to go in, say hello and act the Princess for as long as she needed to. It was so much easier with escape within smelling distance. And of course, now she was an actual adult, her grandmother's control over her had come to an end. At last.

Inhaling, Amber took another step forward, only to halt as her gaze fell on a masculine profile through the part-opened door. A profile she knew all too well: dark hair brushed smoothly back from a high forehead, a distinctly Roman nose flanked by sharp cheekbones hollowing into a firm chin, mouth unsmiling. Amber swallowed. She had spent too many nights dreaming of that mouth. Her heart thumped painfully, her hands damp with remembered embarrassment. What was Tristano Ragrazzi doing here, on her birthday of all days?

Tristano—or, as he was more commonly known, His Most Excellent Royal Highness Crown Prince Tristano of Elsornia—was Amber's first crush. Or, if she was being strictly honest, only crush, despite the four-year age gap and the not insignificant fact that on the few occasions they'd met he'd barely deigned to notice that she was alive. This small detail hadn't stopped a younger Amber weaving an elaborate tale around how he would one day fall in love with her and rescue her from the tower: a tale she had stopped weaving the day she had tripped over one of her grandmother's many embroidered footstools and spilt a tray of drinks and olives over him—perfect hair, exquisite suit, handsome face and all. Hard as she tried, she had never forgotten his incredulous look of horror, the scathing, contemptuous glance he'd shot her way. She hadn't seen him since—and that was more than fine with her.

Amber started to tiptoe backwards—far better to face her grandmother's wrath than His Highness—when Tristano spoke and, at the sound of her name, she froze again.

'Princess Vasilisa is still very young.'

'Yes,' her grandmother agreed in her usual icy, cut-glass tones. 'Which is in your favour. I've ensured she's been kept close; she can be moulded. And of course she has had no opportunity to meet any males. A virgin princess with no scandal attached to her name, excellent academic qualifications, educated in statesmanship and diplomacy is a rare prize and that's before we consider her dowry. She's unique and you know it, Tristano. So let's not play games.'

It was all Amber could do not to gasp. For her grandmother to be discussing her virginity with anyone was mortifying enough but with his Royal Hotness? Her cheeks felt as if they might burst into flame any moment, and not just with embarrassment, with indignation. She was *not* some prize sow to be discussed in terms of breeding! She was surprised her grandmother hadn't mentioned her excellent teeth—unless her dental records had already been discussed!

'Of course, the Belravian fortune,' a male voice she didn't recognise cut in. He had a similar accent to Tristano, only far more noticeable: a little Italian, a little Germanic. 'Is it really worth as much as it was when the country fell?'

'More, thanks to some wise investments as we waited for a Kireyev to sit on the throne once more. But empires have risen and fallen and it's clear that our country is no more, and with it our throne. So we look to another throne, another country in which to invest our money and our blood. Your throne, your country, Tristano.'

Silence fell. Was Tristano tempted, disgusted—or indignant that she was being bartered as if she were part of the fortune, not a living, breathing human? Hope for the latter filled her, only to be dashed when he finally spoke.

'But the fact remains, the Princess is still very young.'

'Let's not be hasty,' the unknown man said. 'The Princess may be too young to marry, but there's no reason not to enter into a formal betrothal. And that's what we are here to discuss. The papers are right here.'

The *what*? She had to be dreaming, surely. Amber barely breathed as she listened.

'I'm her legal guardian,' her grandmother said. 'I can sign right here, with the Duke as my witness. All you need to do is sign as well, Tristano, and then I suggest you take Vasilisa back to Elsornia with you. She can spend the next three years finishing her education to your liking and then, when she comes of Belravian age at twenty-one, she will make you a perfect bride. The perfect Queen.'

A perfect bride indeed! If Amber hadn't been so horrified she would have laughed out loud. She hadn't even been kissed yet;

there was no way she was marrying a prince until she had tried a lot of frogs. Besides, she had her own plans for the next three years and they didn't include being finished off in a castle in the middle of Europe. No, she was going to live like a normal girl. She was going to laugh and learn and flirt and find those frogs and enjoy every moment.

Amber's first instinct was to burst in and tell them all in no uncertain terms that the only person who could sign that agreement was her and she did *not* consent. To remind them that now she was eighteen her grandmother was no longer her guardian—and that even if she was she had no right under US or UK law to marry her granddaughter off, that any betrothal they plotted wasn't worth the paper it was written on. But caution quickly replaced the anger. She had no doubt that her grandmother was capable of taking her forcibly to Elsornia if she chose to. No, better to be careful.

Amber backed away as silently as she could, resolution filling her. She was more than the heir to a long gone throne; she was also English on her mother's side, and it was long past time that she went home. The last sound she heard was a pen scratching over thick paper as she inched back towards her bedroom. Passport, money and she would be gone. And she wouldn't be looking back.

CHAPTER ONE

'ALEX? WHO IS THAT? Standing next to Laurent?' Amber did her best to hiss her question discreetly, aware that television cameras were pointing directly at her and her two fellow bridesmaids. A royal wedding was always An Event, even when the royal in question ruled a tiny Mediterranean kingdom. The kind of event that Amber had avoided over the last eight years—and now here she was, centre stage. But what could she do when one of the three people she loved best in the world was getting married to a Crown Prince?

'That's the best man.' Alex gave her a curious glance. 'Tristano, I think Emilia said he was called. Why the interest? He doesn't look like your type, but he is pretty gorgeous.'

'I'm not *interested* interested,' Amber protested, still in a hiss through as rigid a mouth as she could manage, the last thing she wanted was for someone to read her lips and broadcast the conversation across social media. 'I was just surprised. I thought Laurent's cousin was best man.'

'He was called into surgery.' Laurent's cousin was Head of Surgery at the local hospital and dedicated to his job. Rumour said he was openly praying for a royal heir to push him down the succession within the year. 'Tristano was on standby—he and Laurent have known each other for years apparently.'

'How convenient.' *Not.*

Amber bit her lip as she considered her options. Feigning illness would make her even more conspicuous than she already was—and, she had to face it, bridesmaid at a royal wedding televised for a global audience of millions was already a pretty conspicuous position to be in. She had thought long and hard about trying to wiggle out of the job, knowing that if she was ever going to be recognised, a room full of European royals was the time and place. But in the end she had reasoned that there were only a handful of people who had known her back then.

It was just her luck that one of those people was standing unsmilingly next to the groom, clad in a gilt-covered dress uniform that on anyone less austerely handsome would look gaudy.

She'd changed beyond all recognition, she consoled herself. Like her favourite fictional redhead, her hair had darkened from carrot to auburn and she was no longer a thin, gawky teenager. She'd grown, literally and meta-phorically, during her first year of freedom, and was several inches taller and two dress sizes curvier than she had been in New York. Last time Tristano had seen her she'd been wearing a kilt and blouse, her hair in plaits, make-up free, and she'd tipped a tray of ol-ives over him. There was no way he'd rec-ognise that awkward teenager in the buffed and polished designer-clad bridesmaid. She was completely safe.

Besides, what was the worst that could hap-pen if Tristano did recognise her? It wasn't as if they had ever actually *been* engaged;

he had probably forgotten about that particular debacle years ago, nor could she be compelled to return to the life of a royal. It was just that she loved the anonymity of her life; not even her three close friends and business partners knew of her discarded title or those long lonely years in New York. She'd put life as an exiled royal behind her the day she'd left her grandmother's apartment and had no intention of ever reclaiming it.

The sound of the organ recalled her to her surroundings and Amber lifted her chin and squared her shoulders as the two flower girls began their sedate walk down the aisle, scattering white rose petals as they went. Alex went next, as tall and elegant as ever in the ice-blue and silver dress all three bridesmaids wore, the silk falling in perfect folds to the ancient stone floor. The choir's voices swelled, filling the medieval cathedral as Harriet, with a wink at Amber, followed Alex. Amber quickly looked back at Emilia, ethereal in white lace, her face obscured by her veil, her hand tucked in her father's arm.

'Love you,' Amber mouthed. And then it was her turn.

For the first time she could remember she was grateful for the hours and hours of deportment lessons she'd suffered in her teens as she slowly followed Harriet down the aisle, managing to block out the curious, appraising stares. Amber didn't look to the left or the right as she progressed, not until she finally reached the very front when she couldn't stop her gaze sliding right. Laurent was staring behind her, his face lit up with joy and reverence. Amber swallowed quickly, a lump forming in her throat at the sheer raw emotion the usually reserved Archduke showed so openly, only for her heart to lurch in her chest as she looked past him and met the clear grey-eyed gaze of the Crown Prince of Elsornia. A gaze directed at her, heat flickering in its depths. Had he recognised her after all?

But it wasn't recognition she saw dancing there.

It was desire.

* * *

Tris wasn't a huge fan of weddings, and he had never been attracted to redheads, so why couldn't he stop staring at the flame-haired bridesmaid as she processed with poise and ease down the aisle? Like the two bridesmaids who'd preceded her, she wore blue silk shot through with silver, the blue so faint it was like the reflection of ice, but the colour looked warmer on her creamy skin, set off by a mass of glorious hair set with crystals. She looked like the thaw, warm and welcoming and ever so slightly dangerous. Not that there was anything welcoming in her expression as she met his gaze squarely before turning away. But Tris could see the rosy glow spreading over her neck and shoulders and knew that she wasn't quite as impervious to his interest as she made out. Intriguing.

Or not. He didn't have the time or freedom to dally with bridesmaids, however enticing they were. What he needed was a wife and an heir within the next five years or he'd forfeit the throne, thanks to the crazy old-fashioned laws that still prevailed in his crazy old-fashioned country. With his reckless cousin next in line after him, failure was not an option.

The music swelled to a crescendo and as it ended Tris turned his mind back to the matter at hand. He didn't have to do much, apart from making a speech suitable for broadcasting; after all, the first rule of royal friendships was that you never spoke about royal friendships. Laurent's secrets, tame as they were, were safe with him.

The Armarian Archbishop stepped forward and the wedding ceremony began, following time-hallowed tradition with its well-worn words, repeated by millions of voices yet made unique with each new utterance. Tris couldn't help but get caught up in the spell-like moment as Laurent and Emilia made their vows, promising each other fidelity and honour, love and respect and he was aware of a momentary but sharp envy. Laurent was marrying for love. How many men or women in their position were so lucky? How many got to choose this one part of their destiny?

Not Tris. He had betrothed himself to a girl

he barely knew, not for the famed Belravian fortune but because she had been available, suitable and bred for the role. No wonder she had run away at the very idea. Sometimes he envied her; other times he wondered how she could forsake her duty while he was bound to his. Princes and princesses weren't supposed to follow their hearts—although Laurent was following his right now and he had never looked happier, or more at peace.

The wedding progressed with all due pomp, tempered by the sincerity and love blazing out of the happy couple's faces as they repeated their vows. One lengthy sermon, several solemn choral songs and a demure yet smouldering kiss later, the bells rang out as the couple headed back down the aisle hand in hand, to the claps and cheers of the congregation. Tris courteously gave his arm to Laurent's mother, regal in dark blue and diamonds, but as he escorted her back up the aisle his gaze was drawn to the undulating step of the red-headed bridesmaid, the way the ice-blue silk displayed the curve of her hips, the straight line of her back.

'Her name is Amber,' Laurent's mother informed him drily. 'She works with Emilia, as do the other two bridesmaids.' She paused, eyebrows slightly arched. 'I believe she is currently single.'

'The best man and the bridesmaid?' Tris smiled. 'A bit of a cliché, is it not?'

'A cliché isn't always a bad thing; sometimes it's just that things are meant to be.'

'I didn't have you down as a matchmaker, Your Majesty.'

'I'm not planning on making a habit of it. But you're thirty, Tristano. Thirty and single. Noticing a pretty girl at a wedding is allowed, even for a Crown Prince.'

'But I'm not single. Technically, I am betrothed.'

'Technically is the right word; after all, you're betrothed to a woman you haven't seen for eight years. It's time you gave up on Princess Vasilisa. You deserve a bride who wants to be by your side.'

'We can't all be as lucky as Laurent.' Tristano slowed as they reached the end of the aisle. Photographers awaited them outside

the cathedral and he automatically straightened even more, ensuring his expression was
cool and bland. 'This situation is of my own
making. I shouldn't have agreed to my uncle's
suggestion of a betrothal, nor should I have
accepted the Belravian Dowager Queen's
assurances that she knew where her granddaughter was and that the marriage would go
ahead as planned. I wasted too many years
thinking Vasilisa was completing her education abroad, and by the time her grandmother
confessed the truth the trail was cold. By Elsornian law I am engaged and cannot marry
anyone else, and by that same law I must be
married with an heir by thirty-five. If my
cousin was a different man then it wouldn't
matter so very much.'

Laurent's mother nodded. 'And, of course,
Nikolai is both married and the father of a
son. I do find it ridiculous in this day and
age that an Elsornian Crown Prince cannot
become King until he is thirty-five and must
have fathered an heir to do so.'

'Agreed. The requirement that he must have
led troops into battle and sacked a border

town have become ceremonial only, thank goodness. I don't see my neighbouring countries taking kindly to a sacking. This law is the last remnant of our medieval customs. I plan to overturn it, and to overturn the primogeniture rule as well. But I can only do it with the agreement of my heir, and Nikolai will never agree.'

'What about Parliament? Can they not help?'

'They are reluctant to take the lead. I have lawyers trying to find a way to encourage them, but so far nothing. But this is not the occasion to discuss my troubles; it's a happy day.'

'It is. And so forget matters of state and missing brides and enjoy yourself, Tristano. Flirt with the pretty redhead, enjoy your youth, for one day at least.'

Tristano escorted the Dowager Queen out of the cathedral, posing momentarily for the horde of photographers thronging the square outside the magnificent Gothic building before handing Laurent's mother into a waiting horse-drawn carriage. She would travel alone in the ceremonial procession through the streets, Tristano was to join the three bridesmaids and two flower girls in a larger carriage. An hour with nothing to do but wave to the excited crowds and make small talk with Emilia's friends. Maybe the Dowager Queen was right, maybe today he should forget his cares and responsibilities and enjoy himself. And if enjoying himself meant exploring this unexpected attraction further then what harm would it do? A little bit of flirting hurt nobody.

Luck was with him as he approached the larger carriage. The tallest bridesmaid, Alex, sat on one side with the flower girls, the other two bridesmaids on the bench opposite, Tris's seat between them. The coach driver shook the reins as Tris sat down and the carriage jolted into movement, taking its place in the procession.

'This is so cool,' the littlest flower girl breathed as the carriage rolled out of the square. People were crowded onto both sides of the street, waving flags and holding pictures of Laurent and Emilia, cheering loudly as the carriages passed slowly.

'Wave back,' Amber encouraged them and, at first shyly but then with increasing confidence, the girls did so.

The noise of the crowds and the echo of the horses' hooves made small talk difficult and the occupants of the carriage were busy responding to the enthusiastic crowd, but Tris was preternaturally aware of every shift Amber made. She sat tall and straight, rigid, her face averted from him as if she didn't want to be seen by him, to engage with him. Tris was aware of a ridiculously oversized sense of disappointment. He didn't know this woman, had no idea of her likes or dislikes, her views, whether she had a sense of humour or not, preferred dogs or cats, savoury or sweet. Her studied indifference to him should be meaningless. And yet he had felt a sense of connection the moment he had first seen her, as if at some deep level he did know her. Clearly that sense was one-sided.

By the end of the hour even the flower girls,

Saffron and Scarlett, were exhausted. 'My cheeks ache from smiling and I don't think I can wave any more,' the older one said as the carriage came to a stop. 'And I didn't know carriages were so bumpy!'

'You did really well,' Tris told her and was rewarded with a beaming smile.

The carriages pulled up back outside the cathedral, where cars waited to whisk them away to the palace just a few kilometres outside Armaria's quaint medieval capital city. Here a formal banquet awaited the five hundred wedding guests, to be followed by a much more informal and intimate party for close friends and family only. Tris exited the carriage first, aware that hundreds of cameras were trained directly on him. Now Laurent was married, Tristano was one of the few unmarried European royals left, and the only male in his early thirties. Come Monday he'd be on the front page of every gossip magazine and tabloid, a bull's-eye stamped on his face. Up to now he'd been so busy in Elsornia he'd managed to stay out of the papers, magazines and gossip sites. Being Laurent's best man meant he would be thrust straight into the spotlight, whether he liked it or not.

Ignoring the photographers' call for him to look at them, Tris handed each bridesmaid down in turn, swinging Saffron and Scarlett onto the floor before extending his hand to first Alex, then Harriet and finally Amber. She paused before taking it, her eyes averted before, with a visible breath, she tilted her head, looked him straight in the eyes and took his hand with a cool, firm grip.

Tris was unprepared for the zing that shot up his arm as she touched him, unprepared for the way his breath caught in his throat, his pulse speeded up. As soon as Amber was on steady ground, he let go of her hand. By the flush creeping up her face, he knew she had felt the connection between them too.

But it didn't matter. Laurent's mother could give him all the advice she liked but it changed nothing. He was not free to react to any woman, no matter who she was. He couldn't walk away from who he was, not even for an evening, his duty so ingrained in him that he bled Elsornia.

Tris watched Amber join her friends and head towards the nearest car and made no move to join them. It was safest alone. It always had been. He'd just never *felt* so alone before.

CHAPTER TWO

'HE HASN'T TAKEN his eyes off you all night.' Harriet nudged Amber and not too subtly nodded towards where Tristano sat, his long fingers toying with the stem of his glass in a way which made Amber's stomach clench in spite of herself. She had no idea whether the involuntary reaction was from fear that he somehow had recognised her or because of a desire she barely recognised, one that had ignited the second Tristano had taken her hand to help her from the carriage. Which was ridiculous. It was a light touch, a cursory helping hand, one that had been extended to all of them.

But Harriet was right. Amber had been aware of Tristano's hooded gaze fixed on her all afternoon and into the evening. It was like a caress, dark and dangerous, a wisp of velvet awareness across her bare skin.

'I think he just has a naturally intense, brooding thing going on,' she said with an attempt at a laugh. 'All he needs is a pair of breeches and he would be a dead ringer for Darcy at his most snooty stage.'

'And does that make you Elizabeth Bennet?' Harriet asked with a sly smile and Amber shook her head.

'I have no intention of civilising any man. I want the finished article, thank you.'

'Oh, I don't know, the civilising can be fun.' Harriet looked over at her fiancé, Deangelo, as he leaned against a wall, deep in conversation with Finn, Alex's boyfriend, and Amber groaned.

'I don't want the lurid details, thank you.'

At that moment they were interrupted by a spotlight shining on the dancefloor and an announcement that the bride and groom were about to take to the floor for their first dance. The band struck up a tune, and Laurent led Emilia out onto the floor. She'd changed into a simple long cream dress, her hair loose and

Amber thought, with a lump in her throat, that she'd never looked so beautiful. More beautiful or more distant. This was it. Emilia was married, Harriet would be following her down the aisle in the summer and Alex was spending more time at Finn's country estate than she was at the Chelsea home they had all shared until this week. Her life had seemed so settled and perfect, and now it was all changing. Her friends were moving on and she just wasn't ready.

Taking a sip of the tart refreshing champagne, Amber propped her chin on her hand as she watched the pair waltz to a soft romantic tune, no showy choreography or carefully rehearsed moves, just two people holding each other, lost in each other. Slowly her wistfulness faded, replaced with happiness for her friend and she applauded enthusiastically as the dance ended and the band struck up a much jauntier tune. Other couples began to spill onto the dancefloor and Deangelo stalked over and extended a hand to Harriet, enfolding her in his arms as he led her onto the dancefloor, while Finn whirled

Alex out to join them. Taking another sip of her champagne, Amber tried not to look like she minded being the bridesmaid wallflower.

'Would you like to dance?'

Amber jumped at the sound of the deep, faintly accented tones. She knew what— who—she'd see before she looked up. She took another gulp of the champagne before turning her head. Tristano stood beside her, one hand outstretched in invitation—or command.

'You don't have to ask me, you know. It's not a real rule that the best man has to dance with the bridesmaid.'

'I'm not asking you because it's my duty. I'm asking you because you are the most beautiful woman in the room and I really, really want to dance with you.'

'Oh...' Amber swallowed 'I...' She should say no. It was too dangerous to spend any time with Tristano. Besides, she had no interest in dancing with the Crown Prince of Elsornia. Even if she wasn't afraid of being recognised, she didn't actually *like* him. Sometimes she still heard his voice in her nightmares, sentencing her to a marriage she hadn't consented to, a life in a castle she didn't want to live in.

Only tonight he didn't look pompous or arrogant. He'd changed out of his glossy dress uniform into a perfectly cut dark grey suit, stubble coating his cheeks, his hair no longer neatly combed back but falling over his eyes. But it wasn't his slightly more relaxed appearance that made her pause; it was the heat in his eyes. Want. Desire. For her. Just as she had once dreamed.

'No one has ever called me beautiful before,' she said a little shyly as she took his hand and allowed him to pull her out of her chair.

'I find that hard to believe.'

Amber tilted her chin, reminding herself that she was no longer a schoolgirl, desperate to be noticed. 'It's true. Of course, sometimes I get called hot. Often fit. Nice sometimes. Occasionally gorgeous. But never beautiful.'

Tristano's mouth curled disdainfully. 'Englishmen.'

She laughed. 'I get worse online, but that's

always a useful guide—instant block. There're far too many ginger fetishists out there. One comment on my hair and that's a warning light I always heed.'

His hand tightened on hers. 'What on earth are you doing meeting men online?'

'I'm a twenty-something living in London; there's no other way to date.' She tried to sound worldly and nonchalant, not letting on how soul-destroying the apps and websites were. 'I always promised myself I'd kiss a lot of frogs before I met Mr Right. I just under-estimated how un-kissable most frogs actu-ally are.'

'Do you believe in Mr Right?' The music slowed as they reached the middle of the dancefloor and Amber tried not to tense as Tris took her into a practised hold. This was just a dance, a polite social custom, nothing more, but she could feel every imprint of his fingers burning through the silk of her dress, the places where his body touched hers ignit-ing with a sweet, low heat.

'I believe in soulmates. My parents found each other despite leading very different lives and they were perfect together. So yes, somewhere out there is the right man for me. I just need to find him.'

Warmth flooded her cheeks as she spoke. The champagne and the candlelit ballroom must have loosened her tongue. 'What about you?' she asked, curiosity getting the better of her. 'Do you believe there's someone out there for you?'

Tristano didn't answer for a long time and when he did he sounded resigned. 'I don't believe in true love, no, although seeing Laurent so happy could make a man change his mind, tonight at least.' There was something meaningful in the way he said the last words and Amber's whole body flamed to match her cheeks, her stomach tumbling with heady excitement. She swallowed, moistening her lips with the tip of her tongue, aware of his gaze fastened on her mouth before he continued. 'But Laurent is lucky. Not every prince can follow his heart. It's easier to accept that if you never try.'

'Never try what?'

'Love. The most a man like me can hope for is mutual liking and respect.'

Mutual liking and respect. That was the fate she had been intended for, and yes, she wanted both of those in any future partner, but as part of a much larger whole, a whole that included love and desire.

'Why?' she asked, emboldened by the almost reverential yet possessive way he held her and the intensity in his eyes. 'Why settle?'

'It's complicated.' He smiled then and Amber's breath caught in her throat. The smile wiped away his rather austere, remote expression, making his good looks more boy next door rather than unobtainable gorgeous. 'I'm sorry, that's even more clichéd than the best man dancing with the bridesmaid, but it's true. To explain it I would need to bore you with one thousand years of Elsornian constitution and laws. To be honest, I'd really like to forget about it all for one evening. To just be me, Tris, lucky enough to be dancing with a beautiful woman at a beautiful occasion.

You must think I'm a little mad.' His smile turned rueful and it tugged at Amber's heart.

'Not at all. I know something about expectation and tradition and wanting to just be yourself,' she confessed. For one moment, struck by the relief—and the loneliness—in his dark grey eyes, she thought about going further, thought about telling him who she was, how she maybe understood how he felt more than anyone else in the world, but the sense of self-preservation that had kept her happy and safe for the last eight years kicked in. 'So how about for tonight you forget about it? Be whoever you want to be. Who would you be if you were just Tris and not Crown Prince Tristano?'

'No one has ever asked me that before.' He looked so adorably confused for a moment that she had a crazy impulse to touch his cheek, to trace the sharp line of it round to his solemn, finely cut mouth. 'I'm a qualified lawyer…'

'By choice?'

'Not exactly; it made sense to study law as it helps me do my job. But, to be honest, constitutional and business law can be a little dry.'

'So not a lawyer, something not office based, I guess? Gardener, chef, pirate, actor, survivalist, athlete?'

'They all sound more fun than Privy Council meetings. I like looking at the stars. Maybe I'd be an astronomer?'

'Or an astronaut, living on the space station?'

'I'll imagine I'm there when the Privy Council meetings get too much. How about you? Are you living your dreams?'

Amber couldn't believe how easy it was to talk to Tris; and not just small talk either, but intimate and honest conversation. If only her teen self could hear them confiding in each other, just as she'd dreamed they would, all those years ago. 'In a way. I always wanted to go to university—my dad was an academic and he instilled this huge love of history and learning in me—but, for various reasons, I went straight to work.' Reasons that included not finishing high school, mostly because of the man holding her close and listening to every word as if she was the most interesting person he had ever met.

It was strange to think that in another universe they might be attending this wedding as husband and wife. How would her life have turned out if she had gone along with her grandmother's plans, if the betrothal had been real and followed through? Would they have danced and talked or sat in silence, with nothing to say? It was easy, nestled in his arms, desire thrumming through her in time with the music, to imagine the former, but common sense told her that the latter would have been the more likely outcome. She had been too young, too unformed to marry anyone, even if she had been in love and loved, not harbouring a one-sided crush. A crush that had never quite gone away judging by the butterflies dancing away inside her, and the way her breath caught with every one of his rare, sweet smiles. 'I would still like to take my degree one day. But I love my job. It's different every day, always a new adventure, new things to learn, new people to meet.'

'You are very lucky,' he said softly, but Amber shook her head.

'I made my own luck,' she told him.

'Then you are beautiful and brave.' Sincerity rang in his voice, smouldered in his eyes and as the music played on and his grip tightened it was too easy for Amber to believe him, for tonight at least.

She had told herself that one dance couldn't hurt, had promised herself that she wouldn't have any more champagne, not when it loosened her tongue and made her forget who she was and who she was with. But somehow one dance turned into two and then two more, and at some point, warm from the exertion, and from Tristano's proximity, she agreed when he suggested that he collect an iced bottle of champagne and two glasses and escort her out onto the terrace. It was a crisp, cold February night, the snow still heavy on the distant mountains, the sea air sharp even on the south Mediterranean coast, and Tristano slid out of his jacket to drape it around her shoulders. Amber smiled her thanks. 'How gallant.'

'Not at all, but if you're too cold we can go in,' he said.

'Oh, no. Not when the stars are so beautiful.' What was she doing spending time in a secluded corner with Tris? Playing with fire, that was absolutely certain, because she hadn't misunderstood the heat in his gaze, the way he touched her, held her, as if they were the only people in the entire castle.

It was like all her teenage daydreams come to life, the way he had finally noticed her, seen her, wanted her... To the lonely teenager still inside her, his attention was more intoxicating than the moonlight and champagne combined. Only the reality was better than her daydreams. This older, more mature Tris had a sense of humour she had never suspected, a humanity that drew her to him.

Tris guided her to a corner of the terrace and set the bottle onto a nearby table, opening it and filling a glass before handing it to her. Amber sipped the tart fizzy liquid more quickly than she intended, suddenly shy at being alone with him, even though she could hear the music playing and the babble of voices in the ballroom just a few steps away. 'I've never seen so many stars all at once,' she said, taking another sip and realising her glass was almost empty. She held it out and, after an enquiring raised brow, Tris refilled it. 'I live in London so obviously with all the pollution the sky is never so clear, the stars are faint, but even in the countryside it never looks like this. It's like the sky is filled with crystals, each more beautiful than the last.'

Tristano was so close to her she could feel his breath. 'There's Orion.' He pointed upwards. 'Can you see his belt, and there's his bow, just there. No telescope needed on a night like tonight.'

'Yes...' She barely breathed the word, the heat of him burning into her, despite his thin shirt in the winter air and the thickness of the jacket she wore. 'I see.'

'And there...' he took her hand and moved it, so it pointed to a different spot '...those are the Pleiades, the Seven Sisters, daughters of Atlas.'

'Atlas? He holds the earth on his shoulders, right? Do you think he looks up at his daughters at night?'

'Probably.' She could feel his smile in the way he shifted, in the tenor of his voice.

'Who else can we see?'

'The twins, Castor and Pollux, just there. Twin sons of Leda and brothers of Helen, the most beautiful woman in the world, or so they said. There are some who say she was a redhead.'

She turned to face him, hand on hip mock indignantly. 'I thought I warned you about redhead comments.'

'Ah, but I didn't realise that I was susceptible until tonight.'

As soon as he said the words, Tris wanted to retract them, but how could he when he was standing so close to Amber he could feel every shift and movement, could smell the rich scent of her perfume, when his vision was transfixed by the rich red of her hair?

'Very smooth,' she said, but she was smiling as she spoke.

'Thank you. Like I said, I'm a little unpractised at this.'

'This?'

'Talking to beautiful women. Flirting.'

'Flirting? Is that what we are doing?'

'I hope so.' Tris wasn't sure what had got into him. He never forgot who he was, what he represented, his responsibilities and ties. Never allowed himself as much as a moment off, because if he did then how could he carry on shouldering the duty and the burden, the traditions and all that came with them? No, better to stay on the path he had been put on before he was even born and never look to the left or right.

Only tonight he had allowed himself to glance to the side. Tris didn't know what had caused his uncharacteristic sidestep. Was it seeing Laurent follow his heart, somehow balancing his own royal commitments with marriage to the woman he chose? Showing Tris how his life and the traditions that bound it were as archaic and pointless as he had always secretly thought they were, though so deep down he had never articulated it to himself.

But right now he actually had a choice, even if it was a temporary one-night deal. He could let the moonlight and the champagne, and the undeniable attraction lead him wherever Amber was willing to go. Or he could keep his life simple and turn back to the straight, unyielding path he trod, pick up his burden and march on, letting the last couple of hours fade away, putting them down to a temporary enchantment.

Did he always have to do the right thing? Wasn't even the Crown Prince allowed a night off? Just once?

For one long second he wavered, and then he was overwhelmed by the moment. By the cold air whistling through his thin shirt, the slender-stemmed glass in his hand, the tart champagne lingering on every taste bud, the tang at the back of his throat, the scent of winter flowers mingling with the rich scent of the woman standing before him. By her hair, long and thick, falling in waves, a deep auburn, set off by the silvery blue of her dress and the cream of her skin. By the softness of her breath and the music in her voice, the tilt of her smile and her long, long lashes, lashes half lowered as she looked up at him.

And then he could think no more. Instinct took over, the man pushing the Prince aside for the first time he could remember as he curled his hand lightly around Amber's waist and tilted her pointed chin up so that he could look her full in the face, looking for agreement, for consent, for desire.

Her mouth curved in invitation, her eyelids fluttered and she took an unmistakable step closer until their bodies were touching.

'What do you think? Have I got it wrong, or are we flirting?' He barely managed the words, the light touch of her body flaming through him.

'I think that I hope so too,' she said and with those soft words he was lost. There was no tentativeness in the kiss, no hesitancy as he pulled her to him and nothing but enthusiasm as Amber kissed him back, one of her hands sliding to fist the material at the small of his back, the other to his nape as she rose to meet him. The kiss went from nought to sixty in record time, the first touch igniting a fire and desire almost completely foreign to Tris, who had kept any previous romances as businesslike and emotion-free as he could without making the encounter an actual business transaction. Feelings were too messy for a man who wasn't free to feel. But tonight he was all feeling, every nerve alight with want, consumed by the feel, by the taste of her.

Some dim part of him was still aware of where they were, that anyone could round the corner and see them, and there was enough of the Prince in him still—and enough of the possessive lover even after such a short time—to rebel at the thought of something so intimate being witnessed. 'Come with me?' he whispered against her mouth. 'Inside.'

She pulled back to look up at him. 'Back to the reception?' He couldn't tell if she was affronted or relieved by the idea.

'If you'd like. Or we could go to the suite I am staying in.'

Something he couldn't identify flickered

briefly in her eyes, so swiftly he might have imagined it, before she took his hand.

'I vote for the suite,' she said. 'Let's go.'

CHAPTER THREE

'I KNOW ALEX thinks they're worth pursuing, but seriously, is any account worth this much hassle? Amber, are you even listening to me?'

Amber blinked and tried to concentrate as Harriet paced up and down in front of her desk, but waves of tiredness rolled over her and her head was pounding. Straightening, she stretched, closing her eyes as she did so. What was wrong with her? She'd been feeling exhausted for days. At first she had put it down to the shock of seeing Tris again, but several weeks later she still felt weak, shaky and ridiculously tearful.

'Amber, are you all right?' Harriet looked at her friend with some concern. 'You are awfully pale.'

'I've been feeling a little peaky,' confessed

Amber. 'I think I've picked up some kind of virus, and I just can't seem to shake it.'

Harriet perched on the edge of Amber's desk and lightly touched her forehead, her hand cool and soothing. Amber leaned against it gratefully. 'It's been a while now, hasn't it?'

Amber nodded. 'Maybe I should go and see a doctor.'

'That's not a bad idea,' said Harriet. 'How long exactly have you been feeling like this?'

Amber didn't have to think too hard; she knew exactly when she'd begun to feel ill, as soon as the guilt had hit. 'Since the wedding, I think.'

'The wedding?' Harriet raised her eyebrows. 'Since you and the luscious Prince disappeared off for the evening, you mean?'

Amber's cheeks heated. She had said very little to her friends about that night and they hadn't pressed for any details. The unwritten rule of their friendship was that they never ever pried. All four of them had come into this friendship and business partnership with secrets. Over the last year many of those secrets had been excavated, but Amber's were still intact, including her tryst with Tris. Her friends were all so happy, so in love with men who adored them, she had been ashamed to admit she'd been swept off her feet by the best man at a wedding, only to wake up with nothing more than a note, no matter how beautifully composed. She didn't want to be the single cliché in their group.

'Want to talk about it?' Harriet asked, then frowned. 'No, it's not a question; you haven't been yourself for weeks. I am going to make us both a cup of tea and then I am going to listen, just like you have listened to me and to Alex and Emilia when we needed you.'

'I didn't mind,' Amber protested. 'And really, there's nothing *to* discuss.'

Harriet crossed her arms and did her best to look fierce. 'No arguing. Leave that report and come through to the kitchen.'

Amber opened her mouth, then closed it again. Harriet was usually the easy-going one out of the four of them, but once she was set on something there was no swaying her. She pushed back her chair, closed her laptop lid and followed Harriet into the back of the Chelsea townhouse which was both their head office and their home.

Alex had inherited the Georgian terrace house a couple of years before and with her legacy came the opportunity to make the business they had planned a reality. Their skills in PR, events and administration were the perfect combination for an agency offering both temps and consultancy to private and corporate clients and a year after opening their business was booming.

There were times when Amber still couldn't believe this gorgeous space was theirs. They had decided to use most of the ground floor as both office and reception; wooden floorboards shone with a warm golden glow and the original tiled fireplaces had been renovated to shining glory. Two comfortable-looking sofas sat opposite each other at the front of the room, inviting spaces for potential clients or employees to relax in, the receptionist's desk on the wall behind. Their own desks, an eclectic mixture of vintage and modern classic, faced the reception area in two rows, paperwork neatly filed in the shelves built into the alcoves by the back fireplace. Flowers and plants softened the space, a warm floral print on the blinds and curtains, the same theme picked up in the pictures hanging on the walls.

The door at the back led to a narrow kitchen and a sunny conservatory extension they used as a sitting-cum-dining room and they each had a bedroom on the first or second floor, two to a floor, sharing a bathroom. Only Emilia now lived in Armaria, Alex spent most of her time in the country at Finn's and Harriet would move out when she and Deangelo married later in the year. Their time together had been all too brief.

Harriet directed Amber to sit on the sofa while she made tea and peered into a cupboard. 'No biscuits or cakes?' She glanced over at Amber, her forehead crinkled. 'You haven't baked this week?'

'I haven't felt like it.'

'That's it. Something is definitely up. For you not to bake? That's like, well, there's no metaphor serious enough. Amber, what's wrong? Is it to do with the wedding? With the Prince?'

Amber took the cup of tea gratefully, her eyes hot and heavy, chest tight with unexpected pain. 'Oh, Hatty, I messed up.'

Harriet curled up in the opposite corner of the huge sofa and sipped her tea. 'You don't have to tell me, but it might help. Did you and Tristano spend the night together?'

Amber stared down at her cup. 'Yes.'

'And how did you leave it?'

'We didn't. By the time I woke up he was gone.'

'And he hasn't contacted you?'

'No. But I didn't expect him to. You see, he left a note.'

'A *note*?' Harriet's tone made it very clear what she thought of that and Amber rushed to explain.

'No, no, it's fine. It was actually really lovely.' She still had it, in her bedside drawer. It was a beautifully composed note: an apology, a love letter and a farewell, all in one. He thanked her for giving him an evening where he didn't have to pretend to be someone he wasn't. He thanked her for her kindness. He apologised for leaving her with nothing but a note, but explained that he had no choice, that he couldn't offer her any more than the one night and he asked for her understanding. The part where he told her that she was the most beautiful woman he had ever met, that the memory of that night would stay with him for many, many years to come, were harder to read. For, whether she had meant to or not, Amber knew that she had deceived him…

'Hatty, do you know anything about his situation?'

Harriet frowned. 'Laurent's mother did say something. Doesn't he have to marry and have a son by the time he's thirty-five or the throne goes to his cousin? Have you ever heard anything more absurd?'

'Yes. I didn't know about it during the wedding but Laurent's mother mentioned it the next day. Apparently the cousin is a bit of a playboy and would be a disastrous king.'

'So that's why Tris snuck off, leaving you with a note? Because he needs a queen?

That's even worse, no wonder you're upset. You would make a wonderful queen!'

'Harriet, I can't think of anything worse. I would hate to be a queen. But no, that's not why. There's more.' She took a deep breath. 'Eight years ago he entered into a formal betrothal with someone, but she ran away and he hasn't seen her since. But apparently the betrothal is binding in his country and he can't marry anyone else, unless she formally breaks it.'

Harriet's eyes widened. 'That's absolutely crazy! His country—Elsornia, isn't it?—sounds positively medieval. So that's why he hasn't been in touch, because he's engaged to a missing woman.'

'That's about it.' Amber could hear the blood roaring in her ears, every part of her aching with worry. How had this happened? She'd had no idea that Tris would consider the betrothal binding, that eight years after she'd left his whole life would have come to a halt because of her actions. It simply hadn't occurred to her when she had left her grandmother's house, that the freedom she had claimed came with a price. A price that Tris had to pay. Was paying.

She had to tell Tristano who she really was, now she knew the impact her actions had had on him. She could still summon up the memory of her righteous anger at his arrogance for betrothing himself to a girl who wasn't even in the same room, let alone consenting, but the bitter dislike that had fuelled that anger had dissolved, replaced with a reluctant admiration, and an even more reluctant liking. Every day she started to write to him to tell him who she was and to tell him that he was free. Every day the letter remained unwritten. Amber knew that as soon as Tris realised who she really was, his desire and admiration for her would be replaced by anger. Her friends loved her, but she was also so alone in this world that to have been seen as someone worthy of desire, to have been wanted was so intoxicating it was hard to let go. But let go she must.

'Harriet...' But she couldn't quite bring herself to say the next words. To admit that she was the missing Princess and for her world to change. She took a deep breath but before she could speak Harriet put her tea down and took Amber's hand.

'Amber,' Harriet said slowly. 'Do you think that maybe there's a reason you've been feeling so ill? I mean, you were careful, weren't you?'

'Careful?'

Harriet flushed, her cheeks staining a deep, dark red. 'Could you possibly be pregnant?'

'Of course not!' Amber's cheeks were on fire. 'That is…technically, I guess, it's possible.'

Most groups of girls in their twenties who were as close as Amber, Emilia, Alex and Harriet probably spoke about their love lives in great detail. But that kind of gossip had never been part of their friendship. Partly because of the unspoken rule not to pry, but mostly because none of them, Amber aside, had really dated before meeting their partners and as a result contraception was not something they often discussed. Especially in the practical rather than the theoretical sense.

'Possible, but really unlikely. I'm not an idiot; we used protection, obviously we did.'

'Protection?' Harriet looked steadily at her friend.

'Yes, protection.' Amber really wanted this conversation to go away now.

'Condoms?'

'Harriet! I can't believe you're asking me this. Yes, condoms. Happy?'

'You do know that those things aren't one hundred per cent, don't you? It's easy for mistakes to be made in the heat of the moment.'

Amber swallowed. 'I know that but I'm pretty sure...' She *was* pretty sure they had been careful. No, she knew they had. But they had also been a little intoxicated. Not just on the champagne, but on the night itself. With each other. And it hadn't been just once...

'Amber...' Harriet put a careful hand on her shoulder. 'Before we book that doctor's appointment, maybe we should take a pregnancy test.'

Amber managed a smile at that supportive

we. 'I appreciate your help, but I think this is something I will definitely have to do alone.'

But Harriet was shaking her head. 'No, you are never alone. Remember that, whatever that test does or doesn't say, you are not alone.'

Amber squeezed her friend's hand gratefully, fear tumbling around inside her. Were Harriet's suspicions correct? They made perfect sense. The lethargy, the melancholy, the strangeness in her body. She'd put it down to guilt and something less definable. Not heartbreak exactly—how could she be heartbroken about a man she didn't know? More sadness for a life that wasn't hers, for the wish that she could be simply Amber Blakeley, meeting a man she liked, seeing where that liking might take her, without centuries of tradition and expectation and lies lying between them.

But if Harriet was right then Amber knew that she would be alone. Her friends couldn't support her in this. If she was pregnant with Tris's baby, then she couldn't avoid telling him who she was any longer, and not with a letter setting him free but in person. And all her work to build a life free of Belravia and her grandmother's plans would be for nothing.

But she had no choice. Honour demanded it, and she had this much honour left at least.

CHAPTER FOUR

NORMALLY AMBER WOULD be thrilled to visit Paris. The city had been her first stopping point after she had left her grandmother's apartment, when she had spent a couple of months as a chambermaid in the beautiful French capital before interrailing her way around the continent, finally ending up in London. Her initial plans to go to university had been derailed by her lack of funds and formal qualifications, but instead she had used her hotel experience to get a job as first a receptionist and then a concierge in a London hotel before Deangelo had headhunted her.

She had always meant to return to Paris; the city held such warm and happy memories—memories of freedom, of finding out who she was and what she wanted, memories of evening walks and calorie-filled dinners, of not having to watch what she ate, how she walked, what she wore, what she said and who she spoke to. She would always love the city for those precious few weeks of happiness.

But today she was sitting in the waiting room of the kind of discreet, expensive lawyers who served the royal houses of Europe, knowing that in ten minutes' time she would see Tris again. Amber pressed her hands tightly together and allowed herself a moment of weakness, a moment of wishing she had taken up her friends' offers of companionship and support. Finn, Laurent and Deangelo had all been more than willing to appoint themselves her knight in shining armour, but she had turned down both their money and attempts to accompany her here today. This was something she had to do by herself. This was an appointment only the Princess of Belravia could attend.

'Mademoiselle Blakeley?' The perfectly chic receptionist looked up unsmilingly. 'Please go in.'

Stepping through the open door, Amber looked around nervously. The lawyer's office felt more like a sumptuous library than a place of business. The glossy wooden desk was clearly antique, and the shelves were laden with leather-bound books of all types, not just dry texts. Huge windows let the sunlight bounce in, bathing the room with golden light. It reminded her of her grandmother's study, and for a moment she felt like the sullen schoolgirl she had once been, trying to wrestle her outer self into compliance, even as she raged with rebellion inside.

'Please, *mademoiselle*, sit.'

The receptionist gestured towards a brocade-covered chair by the coffee table at the far end of the room and Amber gratefully sank into it, her legs shaking with nerves and memories. This polite, ruthless, moneyed world was no longer hers, not any more. But she needed the best to guide her through the next few minutes, hours and days and, from all she had heard, Monsieur Clément was the best of the best.

'So, Mademoiselle Blakeley,' Monsieur Clément said in perfect if heavily accented English, 'it is good to finally meet you in person.' If he was at all curious about Amber and the case he was presenting on her behalf, he hid it well. She supposed that was what she was paying for. The lawyer had been suggested by Laurent, who had also offered to pay for him, but Amber had her pride; right now it seemed that was all she had.

She managed a smile. 'Will the Prince be much longer?' She hoped she hadn't betrayed her nervousness through the quiver of her voice.

'He should be here on the hour,' Monsieur Clément said reassuringly. 'I thought it best if we met first, to give you the advantage of the home ground.'

'Of course.' She stilled her trembling legs and tilted her chin. She did have an advantage here; she was the only person in the room who knew the full story. All that Tris knew was that his missing fiancée had shown up at last. He was coming here to verify her identity, and to nullify their betrothal.

And then she'd be free. If she didn't tell him, she would be free.

But how could she keep her pregnancy a secret? They had close friends in common— and she didn't doubt that his people would keep a close eye on her for some months to come. Even if telling him the truth wasn't the right thing to do, it was the only thing to do. If she was going to keep the baby...

Despite herself, her hand slipped to her stomach. As if there was really any doubt. How could a girl who had spent her life longing for someone of her own to love not jump at the opportunity of that, no matter what strings—or chains—came along with it?

She looked up at the silent clock on the wall—only five minutes until the hour. Each second lasted an eternity and yet no time at all had passed when she heard the sound of the outer door opening and the rumble of voices in the reception area. For one dizzying moment she wished she had taken up her friends' offers to accompany her, wished she had the moral support she so desperately needed. But she squared her shoulders and sat back in her chair, every single one of her grandmother's lessons echoing through her head. She was, whether she liked it or not, the Princess of Belravia. And she held all the bargaining chips. 'If you'd like to come this way, Your Royal Highness.'

This was it. There was no going back. Amber clutched the sides of her chair, her knuckles white, and waited.

She didn't recognise the first man who stalked into the room. She guessed he was in his late fifties, greying hair slicked back, dark eyes cold and keen. But the moment he greeted the lawyer she knew his voice, a chill shivering through her. This was the unknown man who had been in her grandmother's study eight years ago. The man who had bargained with her grandmother for her virginity, her hand in marriage and her substantial dowry. Her eyes narrowed even as her breath quickened. This man could be no friend of hers; she was as sure of it as she was her own name. What kind of hold or influence did he have over Tris? But the stranger was forgotten as Tris followed him into the office.

Amber had a couple of seconds to notice the shadows under his grey eyes, the faint stubble coating his sharply cut cheeks and the slight disarray of his usually meticulously combed hair. He looked as if he had barely slept for days, if not weeks. She knew the feeling. She pressed her lips together, not knowing what to say, but knowing that whatever she did say would be the wrong thing.

Tris looked around, his gaze alighting on Amber, surprise and confusion warring on his granite-like face. 'Amber?'

'Hi, Tris.' She winced. *Hi?* It was completely the most inane thing she could have said, but she had no other words.

'What are you doing here?'

'I—'

But the lawyer interjected, 'Please, Your Highness and Your Grace, be seated.'

Nothing more was said for several torturous moments as Tris and the strange man her lawyer had addressed as 'Your Grace' sat in chairs opposite Amber. The unsmiling receptionist carried in a tray stacked with cups, a jug of rich-smelling coffee that made Amber's stomach recoil in horror and tiny little dry biscuits. She set the tray on the coffee table before them and busied herself pouring drinks and handing around biscuits as if they were at a tea party. All the time Tris stared at Amber as if he could not quite believe that she was here.

It wasn't until the receptionist had left the room that Monsieur Clément spoke again. 'Your Highness, Your Grace—Her Royal Highness Princess Vasilisa of Belravia has asked me to speak on her behalf.'

But Tris was on his feet interrupting the lawyer. 'I don't understand,' he said, looking intently at Amber. 'Amber, what are you doing here? Do you know the Princess? Why didn't you say so at the wedding?'

Amber swallowed. She couldn't hide behind a lawyer, no matter how experienced he was, not when Tris was looking at her with such confusion. 'Tris, I'm not Amber... At least I was christened Amber and it's a name I've always gone by.' She shook her head impatiently. Why was she making such a mess of this? 'But my grandmother called me a different name, ignored the name my parents gave me and the surname my father took when he became a British citizen. She could never accept that he had given up any claim to the long-gone throne of a country that no longer existed, that he wanted nothing to do with her dreams of Belravia.'

The confusion in Tris's eyes had disappeared as if it had never been, replaced with a clear, bright anger that hurt her to look at it. 'I am really, really sorry,' she said, aware of how futile the words were. 'I didn't mean for any of this to happen. I just wanted to be free.'

She just wanted to be free. *Free?* Tris could have laughed—if he wasn't quite so angry, that was. Angry with himself for his shock and the stab of hurt that pierced him as her words sunk in and he realised just who she was. Angry with her for knowing all this time and never saying a word, even as he had bared as much of his soul to her as he had ever bared to any other person. Angry at the whole universe for this quirk of fate, a joke played squarely on him.

'Free?' he repeated, voice chilly with numbness. Who did this woman think she was? No matter what she called herself, no matter who she thought she was, she was a princess born and bred, and with that title came responsibilities not freedom. He had accepted that long ago; it was time she did too. 'So to achieve that freedom you did what? You ran away?' Scorn replaced the numbness, biting through the sunlit air.

Amber had been sitting stock-still, eyes fixed on him, a plea in them he had no intention of heeding, but at his words, his tone, her green eyes flashed. Good. She was angry too; anger he could cope with. Anger he understood. Matched.

'I'm not here to go over what happened that day. All I will say is that I don't accept any betrothal entered into on my behalf without my consent and without my knowledge was, or is, valid.'

During their brief conversation, Tris had

been aware of his uncle statue-like beside him, frozen with disbelief. But as Amber finished speaking, her last hurt syllable fading away, his uncle's reserve broke at last and he jumped to his feet. 'Your grandmother had every right...'

Amber held up one slender, pale hand. 'I don't think we've been introduced.' Her voice matched his uncle's in disdain. 'Just as we had not been introduced on the occasion of my eighteenth birthday when you sat discussing my dowry, my future, my body, without *once* considering my wishes.'

Laying a calming hand on his uncle's arm, Tris pressed him back into his seat. 'This is my uncle, the Duke of Eleste. And you're right, Amber. We were wrong that day to enter into negotiations without you. I assumed your grandmother had discussed the proposal with you; I should have ensured that she had before signing anything. But I think we both know I have been punished for that presumption over the last eight years.'

Amber inclined her head, her cheeks still pale, just a spot of colour burning in the centre of them, the warm blush accentuating the cut of her fine bones, the tilt of her chin. 'Thank you.'

'But,' Tris continued; this was not a one-way blame game, no matter what she told herself, 'you were also wrong to just run away. That was the act of a naughty schoolgirl, not a princess.'

Only a faint quiver showed that his words had struck home. 'If you had ever bothered to get to know me...' Her eyes were still fixed on his, as if there was no one else in the room. Her lawyer had stopped remonstrating, his uncle silenced by Tris's gesture. 'If you had ever tried, then you would have known that I was still very much a schoolgirl at heart, even if my grandmother didn't present me as anything but the Princess-in-waiting. If you had bothered to get to know me then you would have known that my hopes and dreams didn't lie in the direction of a throne and a handsome prince.' Her voice was scathing now. 'All I wanted, just like my father before me, was a normal life. That's all I still want. What I have worked for every second since I left.'

'It's been two months.' Tris didn't have the capacity to properly consider her bitter words right now. There was too much truth in them for any quick resolution. He knew that back then uncertainty and the need to find his place in a world where his destiny was so set had made him come across as arrogant. No, not just come across as arrogant; he *had* been arrogant. Arrogant, single-minded and resolute. The last few years, with his destiny suddenly so uncertain, had chipped away at the arrogance, if not the reserve. The only time he had really lost his reserve had been at Laurent's wedding. How unspeakably ironic that it was with this woman. 'Two months since you and I spent time together. I told you I wasn't free; I thought you were aware why. I will absolve you of any deliberate malice towards me before that date. But I'm struggling to understand why, knowing what you know, it's taken you two months to come forward.'

'I was going to write. That's why I engaged a lawyer. I was hoping that you would never have to know who I really was.' Amber's gaze finally broke from his and she looked over at the window, her eyes focusing on the street outside. 'When we… I knew who you were. Of course I did. And I admit I was intrigued. How could I not be? With so much history linking us. But that's what I thought it was, I swear to you. History. I have never once considered myself engaged to you, Tris. And it didn't once occur to me that a betrothal entered into eight years ago, without my consent, thousands of miles away, was still considered valid. I didn't know the entire truth until the next day, when Laurent's mother told me everything.'

Tris briefly closed his eyes. What a mess and, unlike Amber, he knew it was a mess all of his own making.

'I take it—' the Duke finally spoke '—that you are here to revoke the betrothal agreement. That you have decided to do so in person.' Tris could see the machinations behind the smooth expressionless face. His uncle knew as well as he did that they had five years. Five years for Tris to find a wife and father a son. No doubt his uncle had already prepared a list of suitable candidates who would be ready to wed him within the month. He should be relieved. *Was* relieved. His life could move forward at last. He wasn't going to dwell on why he suddenly felt so bereft.

For the first time, Amber faltered. Tris watched her throat move as she swallowed, reaching blindly out for the water in front of her, her gaze still fastened on the window, maybe dreaming once more of escape. 'Tris, I need to speak to you alone.'

'I don't think that's a good idea…'

'Tris, leave the details to me.'

His uncle and the lawyer spoke in unison. But their words were just background noise; all Tris was aware of was Amber. She sat fully erect, her hands folded in front of her, mouth set firm. She was every inch the Princess she was so desperate not to be.

'So be it.' He turned to his uncle. 'Thank you for accompanying me here today, but I need to do this by myself. Actually, Amber and I need to do this by ourselves. If this betrothal had started that way, maybe we wouldn't be ending it here today.'

After a quick, sharp glance at him, his

uncle nodded, standing up and moving towards the door. 'I will wait for you outside.'

Amber nodded at her lawyer who, with a slightly anguished backward glance at his client, followed the Duke out of the office. The door closed firmly behind them.

Finally, they were alone. The silence echoed around them until Tris could hear every beat of his pulse, the thunder of his heartbeat as he waited for Amber to say the words severing the link between them. But after one quick glance in his direction she stayed still and silent.

Despite everything, Tris was conscious of an urge to hold her, to take her tightly folded hands in his, to touch her expressionless face and coax a smile from her bloodless lips. He still couldn't believe it, couldn't reconcile the laughing, flirtatious, fiery bridesmaid with this marble statue.

Nor could he believe he hadn't recognised her at the wedding. True, he hadn't seen her for many years, but her photograph had been on his desk for all that time—an attempt to familiarise himself with the woman who was supposed to have been sharing his life. Not that the gawky teen in the photo bore any resemblance to the woman who sat before him.

'We are alone,' he said, absurdly aware of how redundant the phrase was. 'Whatever you need to say to me, say it. We both know why we're here. Set yourself free.'

In one fluid movement Amber stood, turning to face him, her face so pale she was almost translucent. 'It's true that once I realised that you still considered yourself betrothed to me, once I realised what that meant for you, I planned to end the betrothal.'

'Planned?' Tris tried to dampen down the unwanted hope rising inside him.

'I don't want to be a princess or queen or live anywhere but London. But we don't always get what we want, do we, Tris?'

Nothing she was saying made any sense. This was the woman who had run away with barely anything but the clothes she stood in, in order not to marry him. But, of course, this was also the woman who had shared one of the most passionate nights—if he was being honest, *the* most passionate night—of his life with him.

'No, we don't. But Amber, you always had a choice. Nobody was ever going to drag you to the altar. You could have said no at any time.'

She flushed. 'I appreciate that now but, as I said before, I was very young. My grandmother is very formidable when she wants something. All she ever wanted was to see me on a throne, any throne. Saying no sounds so much easier than actually doing it.'

'Your grandmother is not here now. Say no, Amber. End it.'

'It's not that easy, Tris. You see, I'm pregnant.'

CHAPTER FIVE

AMBER SANK INTO the nearest chair, relieved that she was finally alone, and began to take in her surroundings. She'd spent her teens living in lavish if uncomfortable opulence, but she'd never seen anything like this before. Whoever had designed the suite she'd been allotted in the royal castle of Elsornia had taken luxury and mixed it with style and comfort to create something truly stunning. From the antique four-poster bed, hung with silk, to the brocade-covered walls, her allotted bedroom was perfect.

Almost perfect.

Oh, sure, it had a huge bathroom, too big to be a mere en suite, and the kind of walk-in wardrobe guaranteed to induce envy in all her friends, stairs leading down to an equally beautiful sitting room and study. Windows looked out onto views of rolling hills and green fields with snow-capped mountains rising beyond and the whole suite was tastefully and newly decorated in delicate silvery grey, blue and aqua, priceless antiques juxtaposed with expensive, handmade designer modern furniture. If she was to design an apartment for herself, money no object, then she would probably have designed something very similar to the rooms she now surveyed. But not here. Not in Elsornia, not in a castle and definitely not in rooms located in a tower.

No doubt Tris—or more likely his housekeeper—had thought it was every girl's dream to have a fairy-tale suite of rooms set on two floors in the turret of a medieval castle. But, having spent six long years staring out of the tower windows at Central Park at a world she was not allowed to be part of, Amber knew there was nothing lonelier than a tower.

'That's it!' Amber jumped up and headed to the curved staircase in the corner of her bedroom, which she had been told led up to the large terrace topping the turret. Sure enough, she emerged out onto a spectacular circular paved terrace. A glass roof covered half of the space, chairs and a sofa arranged enticingly beneath, a cosy blanket draped on the back of the sofa. She stepped out onto the exposed stone floor and inhaled the bracing spring air, the breeze refreshing on her skin.

Another deep breath of the clean air helped clear her head and she winced at the thought of how close she had come to a good bout of self-pitying tears. 'No more feeling sorry for yourself, Amber Blakeley. You are no longer a child and you're not a prisoner. You can sulk and feel sorry for yourself and spend the next few weeks feeling unhappy and resentful or you can make the best of it. After all, Tris is right. Like it or not, you were raised to cope with all this. You had eight years of freedom; now it's time to grow up.'

She wandered over to the carved stone balustrade and leaned on it, looking out over the formal palace gardens to the countryside beyond. Shivering, Amber pulled her cashmere cardigan closer around her, eyes blurring with cold as she stared out at the mountains with their promise of escape. It was insane how quickly her life had changed. Less than a week had passed since the meeting in the lawyer's office in France and, instead of interviewing new nannies for the agency as her work calendar said she should be doing, she had flown on a private jet to spend a month in a country she had sworn never to set foot in. Her friends and their partners now all knew her identity and the circumstances that had led to her leaving New York, and they all knew of her pregnancy and what that might mean for Tris and his country.

But throughout the revelations and the confessions and the arrangements she had clung onto one resolution: she wasn't here to rush into a marriage; she was here for a trial before making a decision that would irrevocably bind her life to Tris's and all that came with him. Her hand slipped down to splay over her still flat stomach. Who was she kidding? Their lives were already irrevocably bound. But that didn't have to mean marriage, didn't have to mean spending her life here. There were just too many unknowns.

At least she had ensured the betrothal agreement was nullified *before* she set foot on Elsornian soil. Any future agreement between her and Tris would be their decision to make and theirs only. She had also received a promise that her stay would be both low-key and anonymous; if she didn't marry Tris then there was no reason for anyone outside their immediate circles to know who she was.

One priority was finding out what he wanted to do if the baby was a girl. Would he expect her to provide him with a son within the next five years? Her hands tightened on the balustrade. One child, a baby already on the way, was one thing, but planning a second…? Giving him a son would mean a full marriage in every way. And what if the hypothetical second child wasn't a boy either? She might need to give him a third, or even a fourth…

Giggling a little hysterically, she tried to ignore the heat stealing through her body at the thought. '*Making* the babies isn't the issue, is it?' she asked herself aloud, her words falling into the stillness. 'After all, if you weren't attracted to Tris then you wouldn't be in this situation, would you? Although there's a world of difference between having one baby and signing up to be a baby-making machine.'

She giggled again at the image, her smile quickly fading as the reality of what marriage to Tris would mean sank in. Attraction wasn't the problem. She'd felt its exquisite ache in Paris, despite her embarrassment and the awkwardness of the situation. But from the moment Tris had learned her identity he had been all urbane, polished politeness. Gone was the darkly desirable best man who had turned her head and in his place was the perfect Prince. But perfect princes were not the happy-ever-after she had dreamt of.

A chime rang out through the terrace, breaking into her thoughts and, turning, Amber saw a light on an intercom by the terrace door. Amber walked over, hands shaking as she pressed the button. Was it Tris? She wasn't ready for a tête-à-tête. Not yet.

'Hello?' To her relief her voice sounded steady, showing a confidence she certainly didn't feel.

'Hi, Amber. It's Elisabetta—Tristano's sister. Is now a good time? Tell me if not. I promise not to be offended!' Amber sagged against the wall, thankful that not only was her unexpected guest not Tris but by the friendliness in Elisabetta's voice.

'Now is fine. Hold on while I figure out how to buzz you in.' She pressed a green button and heard the unmistakable sound of a door unlocking and, after giving Elisabetta a good few seconds to push the door open, released the button and made her way back down the curving stairs to meet the Elsornian Princess in the sitting room two floors below.

Tris's sister was standing by the window when Amber arrived, but she rushed over to greet Amber with a continental double kiss followed by a hug. An exceptionally pretty girl of around Amber's own age, the Princess had Tris's colouring, her dark hair worn long and loose, grey eyes sparking with a life and mischief her brother rarely displayed as far as Amber could see. Chicly and expensively dressed in a short woollen dress teamed with knee-length leather boots and a scarf knotted with elegant nonchalance, Elisabetta's smile was warm and seemed genuinely friendly and Amber returned it; it was so good to see a friendly face.

'Here you are at last! I've been dying to meet you for ever, although I quite understand why you went MIA. I am fully aware how high-handed Tris and our esteemed uncle were. Betrothal agreements indeed, the idiots. But I am very happy that you have decided to give Tris a second chance—he's not so stuffy when you get to know him. But I guess you know that, or you wouldn't be here.'

Amber had no idea how to respond. She didn't know how much Tris had told his sister about her visit here, if anyone apart from the two of them—and her friends—knew about their pregnancy.

'Hi.' It seemed an inadequate response to the voluble, friendly greeting she had received, but Elisabetta didn't seem to notice.

'So, Tris has asked me to give you a hand until you know your way around a bit more. You have your own assistant, of course—you've met Maria? Good. Maria is fantastic and will be able to help you with anything you need. She grew up here; there's nothing she doesn't know. If you need anything at any time, just ring the bell here.' Elisabetta indicated a rope pull hanging in the corner.

Amber couldn't help raising her eyebrows at the sight. 'An actual bell?'

'Oh, yes, the walls are so thick that even though Tris has tried to modernise the whole castle, it's easier to stick with the old ways. The Wi-Fi is always cutting out unless you are on the ground floor or up on the roof.'

'Maria showed me to my room; she seems very nice and her English is flawless.'

'Her mother is English and she went to London for a couple of years after school so she is pretty much a native speaker. Her grandmother was a lady-in-waiting to *my* grandmother, but in those days the poor girls were expected to be in traditional dress with hair neatly plaited at all times of the day and night. At least there's a night staff nowadays. Some of Tris's reforms are more successful than the Wi-Fi has been.'

Maria's appointment as her assistant might

be a coincidence, but Amber couldn't help wondering if Tris had purposely picked a fluent English speaker to help her settle in. 'I hear that Elsornian is a mixture of French, Italian and a sprinkling of German; is that correct?'

Elisabetta nodded. 'You could say that, but it's a little bit more complicated. We have many words unknown in any other dialect or language. But don't worry, most people speak English and really appreciate anyone trying just a few words of Elsornian.'

'Hopefully, I'll pick some up. Luckily, I speak tourist-level French, Italian and German...' actually diplomatic-level, thanks to her grandmother '...and I've picked up a little Armarian over the last year, but I'm no natural linguist. Every word has been learned by repetition and more repetition.'

'Any help you need, just ask either me or Maria,' Elisabetta said. 'And when my sisters are home, I know they'll say the same. The palace can seem a little stuffy, so you'll need as many guides as possible to explain the crazy etiquette, who everyone is and, more importantly, all the secret ways we pretend don't exist. Our ancestors were robber barons, you know, so this place is a smugglers' paradise, even if the contraband is only teenagers breaking curfew nowadays!'

'Thank you.' Amber meant it wholeheartedly; it had been hard enough to wrench herself away from the life she had built for herself, but to leave her friends behind, not knowing if she would return, to consider a move to a new country had been almost more than she could bear. Elisabetta's frank, open friendliness was a balm to her soul. 'In that case, there is something you could help me with. I really want to explore the gardens, but I'm not ready to face anyone yet.' Amber was uncomfortably aware that by anyone she meant Tris. 'Do you think you could introduce me to one of those secret ways you just mentioned?'

Elisabetta's eyes lit up with glee. 'I knew I'd like you! Come on, you won't need a ball of wool when you're with me, but don't try this alone until you're a lot more confident—they say there are miles of hidden tunnels beneath the castle and it's easy to take a wrong turn, believe me. Which way do you want to go first? Wine cellars or stables? You choose. And as we walk you can tell me all about what you've been up to and how Tris persuaded you to give him a try. I promised my sisters I would ferret out all the details and I always keep my word!'

CHAPTER SIX

TRIS EXITED THE courtyard and took a moment to enjoy the late afternoon spring sunshine warming his face. He loved this time of year, when the spring flowers began to bloom in earnest and, despite the April rain and the chill that still came with the night, lighter nights and warmer days banished winter. But his moment of enjoyment was fleeting. He had given Amber several hours to settle in before offering to show her around the castle. However, when he had rapped on her door there had been no answer. A few questions had elicited the information that his sister had gone to introduce herself to his fiancée. Which meant the two women could be anywhere, inside or outside the castle.

Elisabetta knew the castle as well as he did, including every secret way out into the gardens and into the land beyond. After all, they had explored the secret passages and grounds together, along with his other sisters, their cousin Nikolai and the other palace children, before his mother and his sisters had left the castle and Tris had had to start growing up. He had never allowed himself to envy his siblings and other companions for the years of childhood they'd still enjoyed whilst he was learning about tradition, etiquette and what being King really entailed. Never allowed himself to mourn the distance that had naturally grown up between them. His father had told him that a king was always alone. It hadn't taken Tris very long to realise how true those words were. The only time he hadn't felt alone in the twenty years since his mother and sisters had left was the night he'd spent with Amber.

But that night had been a lie. Which meant that while he planned for them to marry within the next few months, live together to raise their child and do their best for the country he had been born to rule, he would still be alone, no matter that his pulse speeded up at the very sight of her, that he wanted to wipe away the forlorn look on her face and promise her that everything would be okay.

It wasn't a promise he was qualified to make; all he could do was his best. Do his best not to make Amber as lonely and unhappy as his mother had been, his best to let their child be a child and not a mini monarch in waiting.

His child. Tris stopped. What kind of father would he be? He had no concept of what a good father looked like. He set his jaw and sent out a silent promise to his unborn child; he didn't know how to let go, how to have fun, how to be anyone but the decisive and responsible King, but his child would be more. Would have a childhood full of love and laughter and fun.

The castle gardens were vast, a perfectly designed jigsaw of formal gardens, careful wildernesses, follies, lakes, mazes and woodlands. A man could wander in them for hours and not find the person he was looking for but there was one place everyone visited: the famed fountains that cascaded down the terrace leading to the lake. It was one of the most famous sites in Elsornia, pictured in a thousand books and millions of social media posts. Sure enough, as he reached the first terrace and looked down towards the lake, Amber was sitting on a bench below, the sun glinting off her red hair.

She looked up as if sensing his presence, gazing directly at him, her expression distant, as if she were only half there. Slowly but purposefully, Tris made his way down the stone steps bordering the fountains to join her.

'So, this is where you slipped off to.'

'I know it's a really obvious place to come,' she said, her welcoming smile mechanical rather than genuine. 'But I've seen this view so many times in pictures and paintings, I simply had to see it myself. It's breathtaking.'

'Which way did Betta bring you?' Tris asked. 'Through the wine cellars, or the tunnels that run behind the stables?'

Amber's smile widened, this time reaching her eyes, and Tris couldn't help responding in kind. 'So you know about those?'

'I know all the tunnels,' he said. 'I spent most of my childhood exploring them.'

Her smile dimmed. 'It's hard to imagine you as a small boy, exploring and getting dirty. I'm glad to know you did though, I'm glad to know it's possible. My grandmother always made it sound as if growing up in a place like this was all responsibility and no fun. I don't want that for my child, no matter what the future holds for him or her.'

'Nor do I, Amber.' Tris shifted round to look her straight in the eyes, tilting her chin until her green-eyed gaze met his. 'I promise you, I promise the baby, that his or her childhood will be as full of play, magic and mayhem as any child could wish for.'

'Thank you.' Amber reached up and touched his cheek, the light caress burning through him; he could feel her touch long after her hand fell away. 'Your sister was called away, but I wanted to explore a little more. Would you like to join me?'

'Of course.' Tris stood up and extended a hand to Amber and, after a second's hesitation, she took it and allowed him to help her to her feet. 'Where would you like to go?'

'I don't mind. No, actually, I do have a request. I would like you to take me to somewhere that means something to you. Would that be possible?'

'Somewhere that means something?' Had he heard her correctly? He'd been expecting her to suggest the ornamental lake, the maze or the woodland path, or any of the other places on the tourist map.

'Yes.' She took a step away and looked back at him. 'This is where you were born, where you were brought up; I would really like to see somewhere special to you. Would that be okay?'

Tris didn't answer for a long moment. Somewhere special? The request implied an attempt at intimacy, that Amber was trying to get to know him better. Tris didn't even know where to start. His life wasn't about individual special moments or places; it was about duty.

Only, maybe there was one place...

'Are you warm enough? It's about a twenty-minute walk.'

Amber nodded and they set off. Neither spoke for the next few minutes as Tris led them down the stone steps until they reached the large pond at the bottom of the fountains. Amber turned to look at the water cascading down, a riot of froth and foam and sparkling drops, and Tris watched her, enjoying her evident awe at the famous sight, giving her plenty of time to enjoy the spectacle before resuming their walk. A small stream snaked away from the pond carrying the water towards the lake and Tris followed it, Amber by his side.

'How did you find my sister and Maria?' Tris asked at last as the silence threatened to become oppressive.

'They're both really lovely,' Amber said. 'Thank you so much for suggesting that Maria help me; it was really thoughtful to assign me someone who is both Elsornian and English. And your sister has been very kind. I think I'm going to like her a lot.'

'Betta is one of a kind; her heart is very

much in the right place. Just don't believe everything she tells you; she is an incorrigible chatterbox. And I'm glad you like Maria. I hope she'll convince you that Elsornia isn't too bad a place to live.'

Tris knew a little about the life Amber had led after leaving New York, the months travelling through Europe before settling in London and painstakingly building her life there. The busy, noisy city had no parallels in his small mountainous country. If it was urban culture and living she craved, she was going to find it hard living here. His mother had struggled, had never really adjusted. He didn't want his own wife to resent his country the way his mother had.

'Oh, I'm sure she will. Even from the very little I've seen it's clear Elsornia is extraordinarily beautiful. I love London, but I love the countryside too. But Tris, there's something I really need to make clear to you.' She paused, clearly uncomfortable.

Foreboding stole over him. Whatever Amber wanted to say, he had a feeling she didn't think he was going to like it. 'What's that?' He did his best to sound reassuring. 'It's okay, Amber. I really want you to feel that you can speak to me, however difficult it might seem. If we're going to be married we have to be able to communicate.'

'But that's it. I realised after I agreed to come here that you thought that meant I was also agreeing to marry you. But I'm not, at least not yet.'

A curious numbness crept over Tris. Of course it couldn't be this easy. Of course the girl who had looked at him with desire and light and laughter didn't want him when all the baggage that came with him was included. Of course the answer to the dilemmas he had been wrestling with for the last eight years couldn't finally be within his grasp.

'I don't understand,' he said as evenly as possible. 'In Paris, when you told me you were pregnant, you also said you knew this meant you couldn't end the betrothal. I know you are here for a month so we can get to know each other better, but I thought we would announce our engagement at the end of that month.'

'Tris, I *am* here to get to know you better—and I'm here so you can get to know me. And I am absolutely considering marriage—now I understand your situation, I know that's your preference. But Tris, if you didn't have to marry, would it even be an option for you? Honestly? Marrying someone you've met just a handful of times? Having a baby together doesn't mean we have to spend our lives together, not any more. We can easily co-parent, raise this child together; we don't have to be married to do it well. We don't have to be in a relationship at all.'

Amber's words hung in the air. Would marriage to her be his choice without the ticking clock hanging over him? He pushed the thought away—what was the point in hypotheticals?

'How exactly do you see this civilised co-parenting working? You back in London, me here, unless you're planning to settle in Elsornia?'

She shook her head. 'I don't know.'

'I thought not. So are you planning on granting me the odd weekend and a few weeks in the summer? Is that the plan?' Tris struggled to keep his voice conversational, to hide the biting anger chilling through him.

But, judging by the wary look Amber threw him, he wasn't succeeding. 'There is no plan...how can there be? This is all so new and so unexpected. There's no manual, no guidebook.'

'But there is a law and there is a deadline and I've wasted enough time, thanks to you...'

'That agreement had nothing to do with me.' Her green eyes flashed and his own blood stirred in response to her passion. 'I did you the courtesy of nullifying it, but my lawyer agreed the only court it would ever stand up in was here in Elsornia—and even then there were no guarantees.'

'Maybe. But the fact remains you are carrying my child.'

'And you think that means I have to marry you? Like some medieval maiden, compromised and helpless?'

'Amber, you came to my bed willingly. You came to my bed willingly and in full knowledge of who I was and what our relationship was. Knowledge you didn't share with me. If anyone was compromised by the events of that night, it was me.'

'You? You've got exactly what you wanted. An heir on the way and if I marry you a substantial dowry, along with the Princess your family chose for you. It's all worked out for you, hasn't it?'

Tris bit back an angry retort. He knew how she felt, the lack of control, the realisation that life would never be the same—it was the feeling that had forced her to flee eight years ago. He couldn't let her leave again, but he had to allow her to feel she had a say. More, he had to actually give her a say—and ensure, however difficult, that her answer was the one he needed.

'What exactly are you proposing?'

Amber turned to him, eyes bright with hope. 'I'm proposing that you convince me that Elsornia is right for me and, more importantly, right for this child. If we don't marry, he or she can still grow up with two loving parents, can grow up wanted and cherished and happy, free from all the obligations that you and I know come with a royal title. That's all my father wanted for me; of course I want the same for my child. But it's your baby too. So I need you to show me that if I marry you Elsornia is worth all the sacrifices we both know this baby will make. That it's worth the sacrifices I'll make. That I can be happy here and with you. Are you willing to show me that, Tris?'

Tris had been so intent on the conversation that he hadn't noticed how far they had walked and, with a jolt of surprise, realised they had entered the woods and were close to their destination: the large hollow tree where he had played countless games pretending to be one of the fearless folk heroes he had idolised as a child stood right next to them. And as he put a hand onto the rough bark, realisation hit him hard. He wanted his child to play in this tree, in these woods, to grow up with Elsornia in his or her veins and blood, just as it was in his. All he had to do was convince Amber that it was the right place for her, the right place for their child. Convince her to marry him. How hard could it be?

'How long do I have?'

'I agreed to a month and I'll keep my word,' Amber said. 'At the end of the month I'll be fourteen weeks along, and I'll have had the first scan so hopefully we'll know the baby is healthy. You have until then. Show me your Elsornia, show me why you love it and if you can convince me then we'll talk next steps. I know how important marriage is to you, and why. But you have to understand that I always wanted a very different kind of marriage, a very different life. I am willing to put that aside if you convince me that staying here and marrying you is the right thing for me, for the baby and for you. Fair?'

Was it fair? Tris had less than five years to marry and father an heir. The solution to all his problems was tantalisingly in reach and yet frustratingly far away. But he couldn't deny that Amber had a point. She had to come to this marriage willingly. And if he couldn't convince her, what kind of king was he anyway?

He extended a hand and she took it cautiously. 'Okay. You have a deal.'

He wasn't usually a gambling man, certainly not with stakes this high, but he had no choice. He had to win.

CHAPTER SEVEN

'YOU'RE A REAL natural with children,' Tris said. He sat beside Amber in the car as tall, straight-backed and formal as ever, expression neutral and eyes unreadable. But he was trying; she had to give him credit for that. True to his word, Tris was showing her Elsornia. Over the last week Amber had accompanied Tris and Elisabetta on a tour of a chocolate factory and stood unobtrusively in the background on visits to a hospital and schools. They'd taken her to a production at the Theatre Royale, an impressive baroque building in the capital city, and to several fancy restaurants as well as a trip to a glacier.

But she still hadn't seen beneath the tourist-friendly sites and gloss. She hadn't visited small neighbourhood restaurants or strolled along cobbled streets or shopped in little local stores. The only people she spoke to for more than five minutes were Tris, Maria and Elisabetta, who weren't exactly representative of the normal population. She had yet to use public transport, to order her own drink, to ask directions or sit with a coffee and watch the world go by. How could she decide if this was a place where she could live when she was sheltered from the real world?

It had been an entertaining week, but it felt more as if she was on a whirlwind tour—*The Highlights of Elsornia*—rather than beginning to know and understand Tris more. At no point in the last week had she seen any sign of the man who had made her head spin, for whom she had thrown caution to the wind. They were rarely alone, barely even made eye contact and never touched. She'd asked for time and space and she'd got it, but instead of it helping her resolve her feelings she just felt more and more confused with every busy and courteous day.

'I'm really fond of children; I've worked with a lot, especially since working for Deangelo and starting the agency.' Amber looked out of the window at the gorgeous mountain scenery, so different to the Chelsea streets she usually trod, and her chest ached with home-sickness—for the city, for her friends, for her work. For the life she had worked so hard for.

She made herself carry on, cringing at the artificial brightness in her voice. 'It's strange to think that we've only really been open for a year. Things have changed so much, not just our personal lives, but for the agency too. When we started I was busy with small concierge jobs, sourcing babysitters, doing a bit of nannying and arranging domestic chores. Alex was pleased to be doing the PR for a couple of local restaurants and Emilia's first event was the opening of the café down the road. Opening a new agency was tough without contacts and a reputation. That's why Harriet went back to work for Dean-gelo for what was supposed to be a short con-tract.' She smiled a little wistfully. 'Looking back, I think we all knew that she was in love with him but hadn't admitted it to ourselves. They're so perfect for each other.'

Amber stopped, painfully aware that yet

again she was babbling to fill a silence Tris seemed far more comfortable with than she was. At least talking about her friends was a small step up from this morning's small talk attempt, which had incorporated everything from the cuteness of the local Alpine cattle to the excellence of the palace food to that old staple, the weather. It was a lot easier on the days when Elisabetta accompanied them— or when Tris had to work and the two girls went out alone.

They'd decided to tell people that Amber was a friend of Elisabetta, which meant that she would attract minimal attention, although her presence at Laurent and Emilia's wedding alongside Tris had started some low-level speculation. Luckily, any rumours were still confined to Elsornia and hadn't yet reached the royal-gossip-hungry European magazines. Amber hoped it would stay that way; if she and Tris decided against marriage she didn't want anyone to know who she was or guess at the parentage of her child. Tris's involvement meant secrecy wouldn't be easy but, luckily, she was an old hand at staying under the radar.

Another silence fell and Amber resumed her study of the landscape, searching for a new topic of conversation, one that actually would help her understand Tris better. 'The nursery school was so cute; I loved the song they did. Do you spend a lot of time on visits like this?' Amber hadn't imagined him being quite so visible day to day. Her grandmother's preparation for Amber's future royal life, hopefully on the miraculously restored Belravian throne, had concentrated more on entertaining diplomats and neighbouring royals and less on visiting schools.

'Not a lot, no.' Tris looked regretful. 'Which is a shame because I actually quite enjoy them now. When I was younger I found it a chore to have to try and connect with every single person I met, to shake all those hands and keep smiling so people didn't think I was standoffish. To find things to say that didn't seem stuffy or dull.'

Amber blinked in astonishment. This was probably the most insightful thing Tris had said to her since she had arrived in Elsornia. 'My grandmother insisted I learn how to make small talk; she said it was one of the most invaluable tools in a royal's arsenal. Although, as she spent most of her time interrogating people rather than talking to them, I'm not sure how she knew.'

'My father was more of an interrogator too, which is probably why I found small talk so excruciating. But now my time is so taken up with diplomatic business, politics and negotiation that a day out actually talking to people is a relief. Sometimes visits and openings seem like an indulgence, especially with three sisters who are so popular with the people and who all find it a lot easier than I do, but it's really important that I remember why I do what I do. When I'm in a school, a hospital or retirement home or at a village fair, I can see exactly why it's so important that we have the right deals in place, why I have to spend hours in meetings that seem to have no point. I don't do it for me but for the children who need a solid economy to pay for their schools.'

'I'd never thought about it like that,' Amber confessed. 'My grandmother never really made me see the point of being a princess; it felt like unnecessary rules and restrictions, etiquette for etiquette's sake.'

'There's an element of that, and for a long time I would have put public appearances and visits in that category. Like I said, it was a chore. Something I had to do because, rightly or wrongly, it makes people feel special when someone from my family visits their place of work or their home town or village. Also, it brings attention. If any of my sisters are photographed at a museum, gallery or a nature reserve then the footfall for that place instantly doubles. We know that our attention has an economic benefit. We can't ignore that, just because we might want to stay home and relax.'

'What? You never get to chill out? In that case I'm definitely not staying.'

'Never officially.' For the first time Tris's smile looked both easy and genuine and Amber's heart gave a small traitorous leap. She mentally scolded it and kept her attention on the conversation at hand.

'Okay. It's time to confess—what do you do when you relax? What's your comfort watch of choice? It's been a long day, it's raining outside, you've put on…' Amber had been about to say PJs but thought better of it; this conversation might be flowing easier than usual and she and Tris might have managed to achieve a truce over the last week, but she wasn't ready to talk nightwear with him yet, especially when even the word PJs made her remember in such vivid detail the night when he hadn't bothered with any nightwear at all '…casual clothing,' she managed lamely. 'You're curled up on the sofa, phone set to silent, the remote in your hand. What do you watch? And what do you eat while watching it?'

'I…' Tris looked genuinely discomfited. 'My phone is switched off?'

'On silent,' she corrected him. 'My imagination isn't strong enough to imagine you without a phone or two.' Tris seemed to carry at least three phones at all times, all switched on, all checked regularly and all needing constant attention.

'Usually one of my sisters would choose,' he prevaricated, and Amber shook her head mock sternly.

'That's cheating and you know it. Go on, are you a sci-fi movie franchise man? Must-see dramas? Or do you prefer an epic fantasy series, complete with battles for the throne and dragons? Or is it a little bit too close to home?'

'Honestly? No drama or fantasy series has anything on my ancestors,' he said. 'Remind me to take you to the portrait gallery soon; there's more betrayal, treason, adultery and murder in one room than all of Shakespeare's plays.'

'From what I can tell, my ancestors were pretty bloodthirsty too,' she confessed. 'I don't think my many times great-grandfather got to be King because of his diplomatic skills; I think he hacked his way to the throne. Not that I know much; my grandmother wasn't interested in any of the really fascinating history. She was more concerned with the wrongs done to us during the revolution. But, to be honest, I don't think I blame the populace for getting rid of us. Sounds to me like we were a fairly shady lot, looting half the country's wealth as we left, for instance.'

'Your dowry?'

'My dowry.' She sighed. 'You know, when I left New York I felt completely free for the first time in so many years. I didn't feel guilty about not letting my grandmother know where I was because I never felt like she ever cared for me, just what I represented. I was always flawed, a disappointment. I still don't feel guilty. But I've never felt comfortable about that money. It doesn't really belong to us, does it? I'd like to give it back, only my grandmother still has it and will have until I marry, I guess.' She managed to refrain from adding *If I marry*, but the words hung there.

'You're of age now; it belongs to you and you can do anything you like with it, including giving it back. The only problem is, Belravia doesn't exist any more. It's been carved up and absorbed into at least three countries.'

It belonged to her? It had never occurred to Amber that once she'd turned twenty-one she would legally have charge of the famed Belravian fortune. 'So I just keep it? I couldn't—it doesn't seem right.'

'I'm not saying keep it, but how you'd go about restoring it when Belravia no longer exists I'm not sure. If you'd like, I can do some investigating. There might be some charities or hospitals in the old Belravian towns and cities where the money could be distributed. Or you could set up a charitable foundation; a lot of your people dispersed during the revolution and people continue to be dispersed from their countries today and need a lot of financial aid; that might be a fitting use for it.' He paused then turned to look at her, sincerity in his face and voice. 'Amber, it's important that you know that your dowry was never part of my motivation back then. Although I am sure my uncle thought differently.'

Amber stared at Tris in some confusion, her thoughts in tumult. She'd been so used to thinking of her dowry and the betrothal as one, it was odd to have to disentangle them—and to absolve Tris of being only interested in her money. Plus the insight he showed in thinking of ways she could use her fortune was illuminating, his insightful solutions for a problem that occasionally kept her awake at night. Whether she married him or not, she knew it was finally time to face her grandmother, reclaim the money and do something good with it.

'Thank you. I'd really appreciate your help and advice. It's too important a job to get wrong and I don't really know where to start.'

'You're not even slightly tempted to keep it, to keep any of it?'

Amber shook her head. She might be confused about many things at the moment, but she'd always known that the fabled fortune wasn't hers morally, even if the law said differently. 'No, I know my dad always intended to return it somehow, but his father was still alive then—he didn't die until a few months after my parents' accident—and so he hadn't figured out what to do with it yet.' She stopped, remembering the austere, autocratic old man who'd barely spoken to her in those long, lonely first few months in New York. Maybe he'd been grieving his son; she'd never know. She did know that neither he nor his wife had treated her own grief with any consideration or empathy.

She pushed the memories away and tried to lighten the mood. 'However, I am tempted to see what it's like when you relax. You still haven't answered my question. Is it shameful? You don't have to worry. I'm not going to judge you.'

'Okay then.' Tris's expression was as unreadable as ever. 'Why don't you come over tonight to my rooms for dinner and a movie?'

Go over to his rooms? Amber hadn't been invited into Tris's quarters since she'd been at the castle, nor had she attempted to go there. The invitation was a definite step in the right direction. Nerves fluttered in her stomach. Every small step brought her closer to a decision, closer to deciding the course her life would take.

'Okay, then.' Amber tried her best to look

as inscrutable as Tris. 'You choose the movie and I'll bring popcorn.'

She sat back and stared out of the windows again. This was her chance to find out something real about Tris. To discover who he was when he wasn't the perfect prince, the consummate host or the seductive dance partner. It was a lot to ask of dinner and a movie, but right now she would take whatever insight into Tris she could get. Time was ticking away and she was as far from a decision as she had been the day she arrived. Something had to change and maybe, just maybe, tonight was the night.

CHAPTER EIGHT

'THIS SHIRT? OR this one?' Tris held up first a blue and then a grey shirt and looked hopefully at his sister.

'I thought this was supposed to be a relaxing evening.' Elisabetta raised a knowing eyebrow. 'Box sets and chill? We all know what *that* means. About time, big brother, about time.'

'I barely know her,' Tris protested, trying not to think about how in some ways he knew Amber very well indeed. He knew how silky her skin was beneath his fingertips, he knew the taste of her, the way she gasped, the way her eyes fluttered half shut and she lost herself in sensation. He knew all that and yet in many ways he didn't know her at all.

'Those shirts make you look a little...' Elisabetta put her head to one side and studied him '... stuffy.'

'Stuffy?' Tris regarded the shirts in consternation. They were handmade linen shirts. 'What on earth is wrong with them?'

'You're supposed to be sitting on the sofa, sharing pizza and watching a film. Don't you think you should be in something a little more casual?'

'More casual?' These were casual. They were open-necked and short-sleeved; he'd never wear them in public. 'Like silk pyjamas and some kind of smoking jacket?'

'I was thinking about jeans and a T-shirt,' Elisabetta said. 'But if you want to scare the girl off then go with silk pyjamas.' She studied him, eyes narrowed. 'This means a lot to you, doesn't it? Do you like her?'

Tris refused to meet her gaze. 'She's very pleasant.'

'It's okay; you're allowed to like her, you know. Don't take our parents' marriage as a template; most people *want* to be with the person they marry.' She wandered over to the window and said with studied nonchalance,

'I was talking to Mama earlier; she sends her love. I didn't mention Amber, but I know how relieved she would be to know she was here and that you might be marrying soon. Why don't you take Amber to visit her? Mama would like that.'

'If she wants to know anything about me then she is always welcome here,' he said gruffly. His mother hadn't set foot in Elsornia since the day after his father's funeral and Tris had neither time nor inclination to assuage her conscience by visiting her. He knew the distance between them upset his sisters, but it wasn't of his making, His mother's rooms were always ready if she should change her mind.

Elisabetta didn't answer but he could feel her disappointment as she sighed and looked out of the window.

'What film shall I choose?' The question was a way of changing the subject and it worked as she turned immediately, rolling her eyes in exasperation.

'How can you be so bad at this?'

'Because I've been engaged for eight years with no actual fiancée to spend time with?'

'And because, between Father and our uncle, you've been brought up to be a cross between a monk and a robot? But I know you dated before the betrothal and I know you've had a few *friendships* in the last four years. It's not as if you've never spent time alone with a woman before.'

Tris compressed his mouth grimly. There were many things he and his sisters never discussed—their parents' separation and their mother's decision to leave Tris with his father; the countdown to Tris's thirty-fifth birthday; their father's autocratic ways—and they certainly never discussed the few relationships Tris had had after they'd learned that Amber wasn't studying but had disappeared without a trace.

His partners had been carefully chosen for their discretion: an old friend hopelessly in love with another man, a widow who had no intention of remarrying, a friend of Elisabetta's who was training to be a doctor and had no time for a serious relationship. Trustworthy women who didn't want a long-term love affair, didn't mind secrecy and who would never go to the press. Each affair had lasted for just a few months, ending by mutual agreement when the secrecy became too oppressive. Tris wasn't proud of these relationships, but neither was he ashamed. They'd been necessary, brief interludes of humanity in his duty filled life. If at some level he'd felt that something was missing, he'd pushed that feeling away. He knew that in his world it was all too rare to find true understanding in friendship or relationships. Far better to keep expectations simple than hope for too much and be disappointed.

'I'm sorry,' Elisabetta said, walking over to give him a hug. 'I know being yourself isn't easy for you. But that's all you need to do. I promise, just let Amber get to know you, Tris, let her see the man we see.'

Tris hugged her back, but it was already too late. He had shown Amber his true self and it had made him vulnerable. He had no intention of being vulnerable in front of her again. He needed her and she knew it. He wanted marriage and to be a father to their child all the time, not just on weekends and the occasional holiday. But that was it; he didn't need her to understand him or to see inside his soul.

It was far safer if she didn't.

An hour and two changes of clothes later, Tris was beginning to wish he'd never *heard* the word relax. He'd ordered two pizzas and a salad from the palace kitchen and they sat in a small kitchenette he barely used, ready to be heated up. Elderflower *pressé* cooled in the fridge alongside non-alcoholic beer and sparkling water.

'Get hold of yourself, Tris,' he told himself aloud, pacing over to the open French windows that led out onto his terrace. 'It's just dinner and a film—how hard can it be?'

He turned at the sound of a gentle rap at his door. Opening it, he saw Amber standing there, wearing light blue trousers in some kind of silky material teamed with a creamy-coloured T-shirt and a large white cardigan which she held wrapped about her as if it was armour.

'Hi,' she said.

'Come in.'

She stepped inside, her posture wary, and looked around. 'This is lovely,' she said but her voice sounded carefully neutral. Tris looked at his rooms and tried to see the familiar furniture and decor through her eyes.

His suite of rooms were on the first floor, looking out over the front of the castle, and the large sitting room doubled as an informal receiving room. White walls topped with intricate gilt coving and lined with valuable landscapes of the Elsornian countryside were matched by a polished wooden floor and a selection of antique furniture. Everything in the room was made in Elsornia, the only personal touch a photo of his three sisters on one of the bookshelves. His study was furnished in a similar fashion; his bedroom likewise. His sisters were always trying to persuade him to redecorate, but Tris didn't see the point. He was the Crown Prince, and no amount of wallpaper, photos or cushions would change that.

'Make yourself comfortable,' he said and, with a slightly doubtful look, Amber perched on the nearest brocade sofa.

'This is very…erm…firm.' She wriggled as if trying to get comfortable. True, the sofa wasn't very comfortable. None of the furniture was, but Tris had got used to it. It wasn't as if he spent much time relaxing anyway. In fact, he spent very little time in his rooms, apart from his study, at all.

'Would you like a drink?'

'Thank you, that would be lovely.'

Tris busied himself with getting them both drinks and checked that Amber was happy with the pizzas he had selected before giving her a quick guided tour of his rooms. She seemed interested and asked several questions, but her gaze was a little puzzled and she glanced at Tris several times as if considering saying something. It wasn't until he showed her out to the terrace that ran the full length of his rooms that her smile seemed to become more genuine. She walked from one end to the other, pausing to admire the plants and potted trees that turned the austere stone space into a green paradise, stopping by the telescope set up at the far corner. Reaching out one hand, she touched the telescope lightly and Tris wondered if she, like him, was thinking about the evening he'd shown her the stars. 'So, this is where you spend most of your time when you're alone?'

'I suppose it is.' Tris had never really thought about it before, but she was right. 'How can you tell?'

She shrugged. 'It just seems a little bit more like you, I suppose. Your rooms are lovely, but they're a little impersonal. I could be walking through any show room in any stately home. But out here? This doesn't look like it's been put together out of the Palaces-R-Us catalogue. It looks like someone has curated it with love and care.'

For a moment Tris was so taken aback he didn't know how to respond, and Amber covered her mouth, eyes huge with embarrassment. 'I am so sorry...' she began but Tris interrupted her.

'I moved into these rooms when I was sixteen,' he said. 'My uncle arranged for them to be prepared for me in what he deemed to be the most appropriate style, and I've never got around to changing them; there doesn't seem to be much point. I don't spend much time here anyway. But the terrace is different, I designed it myself and this is where I come when I need to think, to remind myself that the world is bigger than this castle and my responsibilities.' He stopped, a little embarrassed by how much he'd given away.

Amber nodded. 'That makes sense. I couldn't quite believe it when I stepped in... the difference between your rooms and the ones I've been given...mine are so beautiful and so individual.'

'You can thank Elisabetta for that. I asked her to make them as welcoming as she could. I tried to tell her a little bit about you so that you felt at home; I hope I got it right.'

'They're perfect,' she said softly. Amber looked up at him, confusion, doubt and something that looked a little like hope mingling in her eyes. Tris wanted to reach out and touch, to run his finger down her cheek, to bend his head to hers to taste her once again. He wanted to pull her into his arms, to run his hands through her glorious mass of hair, to slide his hands down to her waist, to touch her silky skin, as he had dreamt of every night over the last few weeks. If he did, he was almost sure that she wouldn't push him away; he could almost taste the anticipation in the air.

For all the awkward silences, for all the ways they danced around each other, trying to work out just how much they would need to give and take in any future relationship, for all they avoided any conversation about the night they'd spent together, barely even mentioning her pregnancy even though it was the reason she was here, attraction still hummed in the air between them. Almost visible, tangible, audible it surrounded him every time she was near. And by the way she was so careful not to touch him, the way she sometimes slid a glance his way, Tris knew she felt it, saw it, heard it too.

Kissing Amber, reminding her of that physical attraction, reminding her of how good they were together in one way at least, would give him a shortcut to the marriage he needed. But he'd never been a man for shortcuts; he needed Amber to agree to stay because she wanted to, not because she had to. That ill-judged betrothal needed to be wiped out of history. Seducing her into a decision would be almost as bad as coercing her through a legal document she had had no say in. It almost physically hurt to step back, to keep his polite mask in place, but Tris was used to doing things the hard way.

'I don't know about you,' he said as smoothly and unemotionally as possible, doing his best to pretend the moment that had flared up between them had never happened, 'but I'm hungry. Let's go in and I'll heat up the pizzas. There is a selection of films lined up; you choose.' Tris didn't know if the disappointed glance she sent his way was because Amber had thought he had been about to kiss her or because he was ducking out of their agreement by giving her the choice of film but, either way, this choice was right, safe. And Tris always did the right thing, no matter the personal cost.

CHAPTER NINE

FEELING SLIGHTLY RIDICULOUS, Amber tip-toed along the corridor, unable to stop her-self glancing over her shoulder—although whether she was checking for flesh and blood or ghostly watchers, she wasn't sure. What she was sure of was that there was nothing quite as eerie as a seemingly deserted castle at night.

The dimly lit, thickly carpeted corridor which led from her turret into the main part of the castle eventually gave straight onto the grand main staircase which descended majestically into the huge receiving hall at the front of the castle. But somewhere be-fore there was a discreet door which opened into the passages and stairs the servants used to move around the castle relatively unseen. She had had a full tour the day after she'd arrived but there were so many twists, turns, rooms leading into each other, hidden doors and staircases that she wasn't entirely sure which piece of panelling was the door she needed, and which was a secret way into a bedroom or receiving room; the castle was riddled with secret connecting doors and passages, most of them used either for smugglers or affairs. Tris was right; his ancestors were a scandalous lot.

Pausing beside an engraved panel, Amber could see the tell-tale break in the carving that indicated a door. But was it the right door? More by luck than judgement she selected the right door first time and found herself descending the back stairs leading to the kitchen areas. She'd only had a whistle-stop tour of the palace kitchens, which were ruled over by the kind of temperamental French chef she'd thought only existed in films and who even confident, vivacious Elisabetta regarded with wary respect.

Once down in the airy basement that housed the service apartments and rooms, Amber found she remembered the way to the kitchen easily. Pushing the heavy door a little nervously, she peeped into the simply lit room, her heart jolting with relief when she saw it was both empty and tidied up and cleaned ready for the next day. She stepped in, closing the door softly behind her, and looked around the huge room, with its stainless steel worktops, saucepans hanging from racks and range ovens. It was almost impossible to believe that next door there was an even bigger kitchen used for state occasions and this gleaming, gadget-filled professional room was used just for day-to-day catering.

Tiptoeing over to the light switches, Amber put on the spotlights which illuminated the side benches, holding her breath in case she triggered some kind of alarm, but the only sound was that of her own wildly beating heart roaring in her ears. The night staff had an office at the other end of the basement with another small kitchen for late night orders. She should be able to use this kitchen completely undisturbed.

Fifteen minutes later Amber had filled the worktop in front of her with a selection of eggs, flour, sugar, flavourings and a whole host of bowls, baking tins and wooden spoons. The terrifyingly technical oven nearest her was finally switched on after several false starts, and she had started to mix ingredients together for a simple sponge cake, propping her tablet in front of her and logging into her video chat, hoping that one of her friends might also be finding it hard to sleep.

Amber preferred to cream the butter and sugar by hand, the repetitive exercise giving her the brain space she needed. As she started to turn two separate substances into one she recapped the evening she'd just spent with Tris in excruciating detail. There was so much to unpick she didn't quite know where to start. The shock of his impersonal rooms followed by the relief when she'd stepped onto the terrace and seen the beautiful outside space he'd created. The moment by the telescope when he'd looked at her in exactly the same way he'd looked at her at the wedding, all heat and want. With that one look turning her bones molten, her body limp with need. Only for him to turn away as if it had never happened.

She mixed harder, mind ruthlessly marching on to the disappointment flooding her when he'd left it to her to select the film as if he couldn't share even his cultural taste with her. Choosing a three-hour Jane Austen adaptation was maybe cheap revenge, but he deserved it.

Was it too soon to give up? He was trying, she knew that, probably as much as he was able, but she could not live the rest of her life in bland companionship, no matter how luxurious the surroundings. Her unhappiest years had been spent in the lap of luxury.

The sugar and butter were creamed at last, so smooth a paste it was almost impossible to imagine that just ten minutes ago they had been separate substances. Picking up the first egg, Amber amused herself by cracking it on the side of the bowl and letting the contents slide into the bowl one-handed. She picked up the second egg and at that moment an alert from her tablet showed her Harriet was trying to call. For one moment she considered not answering, despite her earlier need to speak to her friends, unsure what to say and how much to give away. But her need for companionship was greater than her desire for secrecy and she accepted the call.

'Harriet! How lovely to hear from you.' Amber hoped her cheery smile and tone would be enough to fool her friend that all was fine. She should have known better. Harriet narrowed her eyes.

'You're baking?' Harriet said it in the same way that she might have said *You're drinking* or *You're weeping on a sofa watching a sad film*. 'What time is it there?'

'Not yet midnight,' Amber said airily, mixing in the eggs as if making a cake in a castle kitchen at midnight was a completely normal thing to do. 'Why, what time is it where you are? Actually, where are you?' Since Harriet had got engaged to Deangelo she spent a lot of time travelling around the world with him.

'I'm in New York,' Harriet said. 'I've been catching up with the company Alex worked with at Christmas and my report will be with you all at the end of the week, but right now

I'm sitting in a hotel room waiting for my fiancé to finish *his* business and to take me out for dinner. Amber, what's going on? You only midnight bake when you're stressed.'

'I'm not stressed,' protested Amber, sieving in the flour and folding it a little more vigorously than usual. Harriet didn't reply, her silence all too effective, and Amber rolled her eyes in the direction of the tablet. 'Okay, okay, maybe I'm a little stressed. Did I tell you that Tris put me in a freaking tower? Like I'm some helpless princess and now he's impregnated me he's ready to save me.'

'To be fair, it's not as if he knew you were a princess when he impregnated you,' Harriet said, a smile twitching her mouth. 'None of us did.'

'I was talking about a metaphorical princess,' Amber said with as much dignity as she could as the flour flew into the air under her less than tender care and coated her nose and top. 'Dammit, look at the mess I'm making. Besides, I'm not here because I'm a princess, and I'm definitely not here to be saved. I'm here because I'm pregnant and I promised myself to give Tris a chance to show me I could be happy here. Happy with him.'

'And how is that going for you? Or does the large amount of flour currently decorating your face tell me everything I need to know?'

'The pregnancy? I feel surprisingly well, not so tired and I haven't been sick once. It's easy to forget I'm pregnant at all and then I wonder what on earth I'm doing here. I guess that will change next week; I'm flying home for the first scan. Harriet, will you be around? I really don't want to go on my own. Part of me wonders if I'm going to get there and the doctor is going to tell me I'm crazy and there's no baby; I'd like someone else to prove it's real.'

Amber paused. Despite all the problems the pregnancy was causing her, the question marks over her future, she couldn't help but be thrilled at the thought of a baby. Her baby. Her own family for the first time in more years than she cared to remember. No, she reminded herself as she looked at Harriet. She did have a family, one born of love and respect and friendship. Their marriages would inevitably change that, especially as they would no longer live together, but they wouldn't change those bonds. No matter what happened, the baby had three ready-made aunts and godmothers ready to love him or her.

'Of course I'll be there if you want me. But Amber, shouldn't Tris be with you?'

Shaking her head, Amber dislodged flour, sending even more to the floor. 'We're still keeping the pregnancy and, more importantly, Tris's involvement, a secret for now. To be honest, if we don't get married, I'd really like to keep it a secret for as long as possible, until the baby is an adult at least. Growing up with that kind of interest and publicity is not ideal, to put it mildly. Nor is growing up with a meaningless title healthy either. I should know; I crossed an ocean to escape mine.'

'I thought it was your grandmother you wanted to leave behind, not the title. After all, if you know it's meaningless, then what does it matter?'

'It matters because I'm here. Do you think

if I was just some random bridesmaid Tris had got pregnant I'd be living in the castle being prepped for Queen? No way—they'd be paying me off quicker than you could say *royal emergency.*'

'Do you really think that?' Harriet shook her head, her eyes warm with understanding. 'I think you're there because Tris wants you there, because he wants to be part of the baby's life and part of your life.'

'Harriet, he barely speaks to me. There is no trace of the man I met at the wedding, at least barely any trace. I can't see beneath the surface; he won't let me in.'

'Why is that, do you think?'

Amber huffed a little as she started to prepare the ingredients for shortbread biscuits. She couldn't just stand here and chat while her cakes cooked; she had to stay busy. Maybe pastry after this, puff or filo—something tricky which needed a lot of physical work. 'He thinks I lied to him that night.'

'And did you?'

'No! I mean, he didn't ask me, did he? At no point did he say, *Excuse me, are you the long-lost Belravian Princess who I managed to get engaged to without once asking her if it was what she wanted?'* Amber could hear the bitterness in her voice and concentrated on beating the butter as hard as she could.

'Be careful with that butter, Amber, or it will have you up for assault. Okay, he didn't ask you and he didn't recognise you, so why does he think you lied?'

'He thinks I lied by omission.' Amber put the bowl down and faced the screen—and her friend. 'In some ways, I guess I did. Obviously, I knew who he was, but I had no idea he still considered himself betrothed to me. If I had, I wouldn't have danced with him, I wouldn't have slept with him. I wouldn't have complicated things so badly.'

Harriet's nod was full of understanding. After all, she and Deangelo had had to find their way from desire towards love. 'Amber, tell me to mind my own business, but *why* did you sleep with him? Knowing who he was, knowing he is the reason you left your grandmother's house before graduating. I'm not judging,' she added hastily as Amber picked the bowl back up.

The heat in Amber's face had nothing to do with the vigorous beating of butter and the newly added sugar and everything to do with embarrassment. Harriet had just said what they were all thinking, herself too, no doubt Tris as well. What *had* she been thinking?

'At first I was terrified he would recognise me and, although there's no way anyone could make me go back to my grandmother or force me into marriage, for a few moments I was a terrified schoolgirl again, hearing her future planned out for her with no say and no way out except to run. When I realised he had no idea who I was, I was curious I suppose, curious how my life might have turned out if I hadn't had the strength to disappear. And—' the heat of her face intensified '—the truth is, when I was a teenager I had a huge crush on him, although he looked at me as if I was nothing more exciting than a cockroach. When it became clear he was attracted to me it went to my head. I felt powerful after all those years of feeling powerless. It was more intoxicating than the champagne. He wanted me not because I was a princess and a means to a throne and a fortune, but me, Amber Blakeley, and that night it seemed like I could see into his soul.'

She stopped, unable to believe the words that had just spilled out of her, unable to believe their truth, but when she finally got the courage to look at Harriet she didn't see surprise or condemnation, but understanding—and confirmation—as if Harriet had suspected how Amber felt all along. But how could she when Amber herself hadn't known?

'I came here because I thought there was a connection,' she said quietly. 'But I was wrong. I didn't see into his soul. I just fancied him, that was all. I made a huge mistake, and now I don't know what to do for the best. Apart from bake.'

Tris paused at the closed kitchen door, unsure whether to open it or not. When he'd received the call telling him that Amber had been in the kitchen for almost an hour he had immediately got dressed and left his apartments to come and find her. It wasn't that he was worried she was hurt but he had noticed a curiously blank look in her eyes when she had left earlier. He had failed her. He was fully aware of that.

Tapping lightly on the door, he waited for an answer and, when none was forthcoming, he carefully turned the handle and pushed the door open just a fraction. His immediate attention was caught by the mass of bowls, cutlery and baking paraphernalia on the worktop opposite, only for the whole scene to fade as he heard Amber speak.

'I just fancied him, that was all. I made a huge mistake, and now I don't know what to do for the best.'

Something brittle, something in the region of his heart, twisted and cracked. She had made a mistake, of course she had. One of the things he respected about Amber was her refreshing honesty when it came to his title and position. The knowledge that she'd chosen him not because of what he was but because of who he was. But she'd chosen him for one night only, not for a lifetime, and now she realised that the night they had shared was a mistake. Carefully, silently he closed the door and took a step back.

He should turn around, go back to his apartments, the soulless, lifeless apartments Amber had been so unimpressed by earlier, go back to bed and forget he had overheard anything. Tomorrow they could resume their slow, stately, courteous courtship and he could rely on Amber's upbringing and sense of fairness to make up for his inability to woo her. To let her in. That was the safest option, the option that gave him the best chance at his desired outcome.

He inhaled slowly.

His desired outcome, the right outcome, was a sensible marriage where both parties knew exactly what they wanted from the union. A marriage giving him the son he needed and a consort willing and capable to put Elsornia first. Even if Amber hadn't been his betrothed, wasn't raised for a situation such as this, she would still be suitable. She was warm, approachable, hard-working with an innate sense of responsibility. And she was carrying his child. What else did he need? He certainly didn't need to remember the night when her smile was full of promise, her eyes full of stars, and she made him feel like a man, not a prince. And that was an outcome best achieved by pretending he had seen and heard nothing.

But the desolate ring in her voice echoed through him. He had let her down tonight, withheld himself, just as he withheld himself from everyone, even his sisters. It was safer that way. A king was always alone; his father had taught him well. But he wasn't King yet, just a prince, and without Amber and the child she carried maybe he never would be.

Without stopping to think, Tris reached for the door handle again and this time made a show of fumbling as he turned it, making plenty of noise as he pushed the door open. Amber turned, surprise mingling with guilt on her face as she closed her tablet. Dressed in pyjama bottoms, a soft cashmere hoodie, with her hair scraped off her face, no make-up and a liberal dusting of flour over her hair, cheeks and front she looked more like the teenager he had first met than the desirable bridesmaid or the elegant companion of the last week. The girl he owed a duty of care to, a girl he had let down.

'Tris! What are you doing here?'

Tris thought quickly. He didn't want Amber to feel that she was under surveillance or that she couldn't wander wherever she wished. 'I wanted a snack.'

'A snack?' One arched eyebrow indicated her disbelief. 'Isn't there an army of night staff ready to bring you whatever you need?'

'A snack and a stroll,' he amended, his urbane smile daring her to question his word. 'I thought it might help me sleep. But the real question is, what are you doing?'

'What do you think I'm doing?' Her words and tone were sassy, but her expression was anxious and still a little guilty. 'I'm baking. Can't you tell?'

Even without the flour and all the ingredients and bowls scattered around, the enticing aroma wafting from the oven would have been a gigantic clue. 'Something gave me that impression, I'm more interested in why. You often bake at midnight?'

'I wouldn't go so far as to say often, but it's not unusual. I bake when I need to think. Like you and astronomy, I suppose.'

With an effort, Tris didn't react to her words. He shouldn't be surprised at her deduction. After all, not only had she seen the telescope on his balcony, but he had used the stars to seduce her. He just hadn't realised that she'd understood that astronomy wasn't just a hobby but a way of centring himself. A way of reminding himself that the universe was bigger than one almost-king and his small, beloved and all-consuming country.

'What are you making?'

'Nothing at all complicated, just a plain sponge and some shortbread. But I was thinking of making pastry or something with dough. My mind is still not settled; I need something more absorbing.'

'A cake seems pretty complicated to me,' Tris said and was rewarded with a genuine if pitying smile.

'It's just mixing things together in the right

quantities in the right order, nothing complicated about that. It's no different to making
little cakes or tarts as a child.'

'Is that what you did? Is that how you
learned to bake?'

Amber looked surprised. 'Of course, didn't
you?'

Tris picked up an egg. 'Baking isn't really
part of a king's curriculum.'

'No, but you must have at least made little
fairy cakes, rubbery and almost inedible but
your parents had to eat them anyway?'

Tris tried to imagine his austere, remote
father sampling any cooking his children
brought him, but his imagination failed him.
'The girls may have, but I doubt it. I don't remember my mother ever setting foot in the
kitchen. Of course they spent most of their
time with her when she moved out of the castle and into the lakeside villa. It's possible
they baked then, but not here. We were never
encouraged to hang around the kitchens here.'

'It's never too late to learn.' Amber handed
him a bowl and Tris automatically took it,

placing the egg carefully inside. 'What do you want to bake? I'll show you.'

'What, now? It's after midnight.'

'Why not? Have you got anything better to do?'

Tris automatically opened his mouth to say of course he had something better to do, but then he looked over at Amber, her hair beginning to fall out of its messy bun, tendrils framing her heart-shaped face, hope in her large green eyes. He'd been unable to let her in earlier, hadn't known how to do anything but keep her at arm's length, but maybe he could—maybe he should—try harder.

'I guess not. Okay, I'm all yours.'

CHAPTER TEN

AMBER STARED AT TRIS, her mouth dry. She hadn't really expected him to agree. The thought of the usually immaculate Tris in an apron, hands covered in flour, was so incongruous her mind couldn't conjure up an image.

'Great.' Incongruous or not, this was an opportunity she couldn't throw away. Wasn't she down here, baking furiously and complaining to Harriet, because Tris was resolutely keeping her at arm's length?

'Great,' Tris repeated. 'What do I do first?'

Amber eyed Tris assessingly. He was still wearing the beautiful grey shirt and well cut tailored trousers he'd been wearing earlier. For a prince the outfit might count as casual but in an already flour-filled kitchen he was dangerously overdressed.

'An apron might be a good start. There're a couple hanging up over there.'

The beep of the timer interrupted her, and Amber busied herself with taking the cakes out of the oven and replacing them with the shortbread before turning to Tris.

'Where shall we start? Cake, cookies, pies, bread—or would you like to go straight for the jugular and have a go at a soufflé?'

'Tempting as a soufflé sounds, I think I'll stick with something simple for now.'

'That sounds like a good plan.' Amber tried to ignore noticing just how close Tris was standing, tried to ignore his distinctly masculine scent, the way his proximity made the hairs on her wrists rise and her pulse beat just a little faster. 'A simple loaf cake. There are some lemons over there; how do you feel about lemon drizzle?'

'I'm not sure I've ever tried lemon drizzle, but I'm willing to give it a go.'

'You've never tried lemon drizzle? How is that even possible? It's a good thing I came along.' She paused. 'But if I'm going to teach you to bake, I need something in return.'

'That seems fair. Name your price.'

'Have you never read a fairy tale? You should never just invite anyone to name their price. What if I asked for your soul, or your firstborn child…?' Her voice trailed off, aware that his firstborn child was indeed in her possession. She rallied. 'Don't worry, I'm not going to ask for anything lasting. But in return for the lesson I'm going to ask you a question and you are going to promise to tell me the truth as best you can.'

Tris didn't respond for a long moment, his smile still in place but his expression the shuttered one she was beginning to know all too well.

'I did tell you to name your price, didn't I? Okay, ask away.'

Amber fumbled for a glass of water, her throat suddenly dry. This was it, this was what she'd been wanting. The opportunity to get to know the real Tris, not the public persona he presented.

'First things first, you need to get your ingredients together. Right, I hope you've got a good memory. You want two hundred and twenty-five grams of butter…' She reeled off a long list of ingredients and first steps. 'Got all that? I'm going to put my favourite recipe on the tablet for you to follow, but yell with any questions. Okay?'

'Yes, chef.' Tris gave a cheeky grin and half salute as he started to gather all the ingredients she'd specified together on the workbench next to hers and she couldn't help but return his smile, warmed by his informality—and the ridiculousness of the starched white apron covering his shirt and trousers.

Humming to herself, Amber started to tidy up and prepare the things she needed to sandwich the cake she'd already made while supervising Tris and thinking about what to ask him. She felt like a princess in a fairy tale with only three chances to get her questions right before he disappeared in a wisp of smoke, leaving her no further forward than she was right now.

'My mother was a doctor.' Amber hadn't meant to say that; she hadn't meant to talk about herself at all. But now she'd started it felt easier than simply interrogating Tris.

She needed to learn about him, but maybe he needed to learn about her as well. 'That's how she met my dad. He fell off his bike and she was the surgeon who operated on his knee. I don't think marriage or kids were really on her radar at all. I remember her telling me that as a scientist she absolutely didn't believe in love at first sight, but when she did her rounds to check on Dad after his operation she could barely concentrate on her notes. Of course, ethically, she couldn't do anything about it, but luckily Dad felt the same way and once he was discharged he came back with a thank you card and asked her out. They got married a year later and I showed up a year after that.'

She stared down at her hands, her eyes blurring as she remembered her sweet, slightly eccentric parents. 'Dad was in his forties, Mum almost there. I think it was a shock to both of them, becoming parents. They were both so dedicated to their jobs, but I always felt loved and wanted. That made it easier later, after they died. Anyway, my mum loved to bake. It was how she de-stressed. One of my earliest memories is being given pastry to play with at the table while she made pies. As you can imagine, my grandmother did *not* encourage the habit; baking is very much something that servants did. But her cook used to teach me secretly, as did my favourite doorman's wife on the rare occasions I could sneak away. I'm not sure I could have survived that penthouse if I couldn't bake.'

Amber couldn't believe she had just blurted out so much. But when she looked up at Tris she saw his gaze fastened on hers, empathy warming his grey eyes. 'Your parents sound lovely,' he said softly, and she nodded, her heart and throat too full to speak. 'It must have been really tough for you when they died.'

'It was.' Amber laid the back of her hand onto one of the sponges, relieved that it was cool enough for her to start whipping the cream. She couldn't just stand here blethering on about a past she never really spoke to anyone about. But she also wanted honesty from Tris, and that meant being honest in return. 'I was devastated. Even if my grandparents had been different, I would still have found the whole situation inconceivably difficult. Maybe, in a way, the sheer surrealism of what happened next shielded me from the worst of my grief. My life changed so absolutely that I think I was numb for many, many months. Moving from a small village where I was just Amber Blakeley, normal middle-class girl living a normal middle-class life, to New York, where I was Vasilisa Kireyev, Crown Princess of Belravia and heir to a vast fortune, would have been the most discombobulating thing ever, even if I hadn't been dealing with my parents' deaths.'

Amber swallowed and concentrated on the cream so she didn't have to look at the pity on Tris's face. She'd never really talked about the car accident that had stolen her parents from her. Her grandparents must have grieved in their own way, but Amber had never been encouraged to discuss her feelings or offered counselling. One of the hardest things about opening the Pandora's box that contained her past was realising how much she still had to come to terms with the loss.

'My grandfather died just a few months after I moved to New York and so it was just my grandmother and me. It was hard. She was hard. Leaving the house my parents bought when I was a baby, all my memories, was bad enough, but the sheltered existence she insisted on... I felt like I was imprisoned in that tower. My grandmother would never let me out unaccompanied, wouldn't allow me to select my friends or my hobbies. I used to stand at the window and stare out at Central Park, at the joggers and the dog walkers and the kids and wish that someone would rescue me.'

Amber could feel her cheeks heating; there was no way she was letting Tris know that the first time she'd seen him she'd cast him in the role of knight in shining armour. She'd spent way too many long, lonely evenings conjuring up tales of rescue, some actually including Tris on a white horse. She busied herself ladling cream into a bowl and fetching the jam. Anything not to look at him.

'Did you know your grandmother well? Before you went to live with her?'

Amber shook her head. 'I'd met her twice, I think. She never came to the house and we never visited her in New York but once or twice she came to London and we met her for dinner in whichever fancy hotel she was gracing with her royal presence. My grandfather never accompanied her. Truth is, my dad barely ever mentioned the whole royal thing. He changed his name when he went to boarding school in his teens as a security measure, but liked being plain Stephen Blakeley so much he just stayed as him; he said he was really proud of his doctor title because he'd earned it with his PhD, but a royal title just meant his ancestor had been more of a thug than the next man.' She managed a smile. 'Anyway, I didn't mean to bore you with the life and times of Amber Blakeley; I was clumsily trying to tell you why baking is important to me. It's not just the creative part of it or the fact that I really, really like cake, but it's tied into the happiest memories of my childhood.'

* * *

While Amber spoke, Tris had been busy following the instructions she had brought up for him on her tablet. It was oddly soothing combining the ingredients, seeing all the disparate parts turn into a creamy whole. Meanwhile, with practised ease, Amber was whipping cream, smoothing jam onto a cake and removing tantalisingly aromatic biscuits from the oven, her every move graceful as if she were in a well-known dance, one whose steps he could barely comprehend. He was glad of something to do with his hands and something to focus on completely as she completely un-self-pityingly laid bare the reality of her childhood. It must have been much harder for her, those long lonely teenage years, after knowing such warmth and happiness, than it had been for him, raised solely for duty and responsibility.

'Okay, let me take a look,' Amber said, coming to stand next to him. She smelt of vanilla and sugar and warmth. How did she have so much light and optimism after so much darkness? 'That's not bad at all. Now, pour it into the tin and smooth out the top and then you can pop it into the oven. A loaf cake takes about forty minutes to bake, so we'll have to think of something else to make while we are waiting. Something quick or we'll be here all night and I want to tidy up and hide all evidence long before the kitchen staff turn up.'

'Or we could eat some of that amazing-looking cake instead,' Tris suggested.

'We could. Of course, for that I need a cup of tea. You can take the girl out of England, but you can't stop her craving her daily cuppa.'

Five minutes later Amber had managed to find a brand of tea she was happy with and made herself a large cup, Tris opting for a glass of wine instead. Two generous slices of the cake she'd made lay on plates before them as they perched on stools side by side. He couldn't remember when he'd last had such an informal meal, even when it was a simple snack. Even the pizza he had painstakingly heated up earlier had been served on a table, already laid with silverware and linen.

Amber took a sip of her tea and then took an audible breath, as if trying to find the courage to speak. 'Thank you for listening just now. I've never actually said any of that to anybody before. Not even to myself really. At the time it was all too much and afterwards I was just so relieved to be away. In a funny way, I should thank you for that as well. I mean I always meant to leave as soon as I'd graduated from high school, but you gave me the impetus to start living my own life the way I wanted to.'

'And was it? The life you wanted?'

Amber forked a portion of cake, looking thoughtful as she did so. 'It wasn't the life I planned,' she said at last. 'I had wanted to study history like my dad. Maybe even become an academic like him. But actually I loved being a concierge, I loved working for Deangelo and setting up the agency was just so exciting and empowering; it felt like I was in the right place at the right time doing the right thing for me.'

Tris laid down his fork. All that had changed thanks to him. Amber was no longer in the right place for her, even if she was exactly where he needed her to be. Victory tasted bitter, no matter how delicious the cake.

But Amber didn't look bitter; instead she leaned back on her stool and pointed her fork at him. 'You know, this whole baking experience was meant to be a chance for me to ask you some questions and instead all I've done is talk about myself. That's partly my fault, but don't think I haven't noticed you encouraging me to carry on. You don't get away with it that easily, Your Royal Highness.'

Tris sipped his wine and tried to look as nonchalant as Amber did. 'I was just showing an interest in everything you said,' he protested. 'Ask away. I've got nothing to hide.'

Her snort was frankly disbelieving. 'In that case, tell me your favourite film.'

Tris took another sip of his wine and another mouth of cake, barely tasting it. Of course she wasn't going to let that one lie and why should she? He knew she'd noticed his earlier evasion. 'I don't really have a favourite film,' he confessed and watched her eyebrows shoot up in surprise.

'Everybody has a favourite film. Or at least several films they'd find it really hard to decide between; is that what you mean?'

'Not really.' Tris broke off a piece of cake and crumbled it with his fork. 'I just haven't seen a lot of films. I attend premieres on the rare occasion Elsornia hosts them but settling down and watching one isn't something I do for fun.'

'More of a box set guy? We always have a box set or two on the go at the house. Usually some kind of reality guilty pleasure for when we're all exhausted and a dark, twisty detective series for the rare occasions when we are alert.'

'Actually, I don't really watch much TV at all. I don't read fiction either or listen to much music.' He might as well pre-empt the inevitable next questions before Amber asked him to name his favourite song or book.

'Not into culture?' Amber's eagerness had faded, her body language on high alert as she imperceptibly leaned away from him. 'Not everyone is, I suppose.' But her voice was full of doubt.

'It's not so much that I'm not into it; it's more that I don't really know what I like. Taking time out to read, to listen to music or to watch TV wasn't really encouraged. My father thought activities should be improving. Obviously, a good history documentary or non-fiction book would be tolerated, a visit to the royal box to watch opera or ballet or even live theatre was work and therefore acceptable, but that was it.'

'But your sisters... I was talking to Elisabetta about a show we both liked just yesterday.'

'It was different for my sisters; they lived with my mother, whereas I was brought up here with my father and tutor. My father took my training very seriously; that's why he didn't send me to school and wanted to make sure I used every hour wisely.' Tris deliberately took a large gulp of wine and pushed his plate away. Amber had been so candid with him earlier, had even confessed that she had told him things she'd never told anyone else before, and her trust in him was the greatest gift he'd ever been given. But he didn't know how to return it, didn't know how to put into words how it had been, growing up here on his own with the weight of expectation crushing him, feeling guilty for missing his mother and sisters, guilty for resenting his father and the regime imposed on him.

He started as Amber laid a warm hand on his, her touch shooting through him. 'Tris, you've been an adult for a long time now; your father died a decade ago. Haven't you ever been tempted to do things another way? To veg out and binge on a box set or a really good book?'

'Tempted? Of course, all the time. But my father was right; there's always too much to do to relax. Duty comes first. Besides—' honesty compelled him to continue '—like I said earlier, I don't know where to start. Even if I had the time, I wouldn't know what to choose.' Tris stopped, embarrassed. Not knowing was weakness and weakness was intolerable in a king. He didn't want to look at Amber and see pity in her face.

Amber jumped to her feet and gathered up the plates and her cup. 'I can see I'm going to have my work cut out,' she said. 'Not only am I going to have to teach you to bake, but I'm going to have to teach you to relax as well. I'm going to need to up my rates. My agency is very expensive, you know, and right now you're getting a lot of hours.'

'Oh, I know how to relax,' Tris said, and Amber laughed.

'You're going to have to prove that to me, I'm afraid.' She smiled over at him and their eyes held. Despite, or maybe because of, the lateness of the hour, the confidences shared, Tris could feel his pulse begin to race, the blood rushing around his body heightening every nerve, every sinew, every muscle. He couldn't take his gaze off Amber as her smile wavered and disappeared as she visibly swallowed. He'd desired the elegant bridesmaid in her silk and jewels, but he wanted this tousled, flour-spattered baking goddess so much more. She wasn't an illusion, a dream, a siren ready to seduce and be seduced, but so real she made his heart and body ache, thrilling and terrifying in equal measure.

Slowly, purposefully, Tris got to his feet,

the invisible thread connecting their gazes, their bodies, tightening. 'I can absolutely prove it to you. Any time.' He took a step closer and then another as Amber stood still, as if paralysed. There was no champagne to fuel him, no violins serenading them, no stars to witness, just two of them in the dimly lit kitchen, the scent of vanilla and lemon and sugar permeating the air.

All Tris knew was that he had mishandled the situation from the moment he'd set foot in the lawyer's office in Paris. He'd allowed hurt and anger to guide him, keeping Amber at a dignified arm's length, too proud to woo her. He'd blamed her for deceiving him without ever considering her reasons. He shouldn't have had to listen to her starkly told tale of loneliness to trust her. He'd been in the wrong all those years ago and he was in the wrong now. Elisabetta was right; if he wasn't careful, he was going to give Amber every reason to walk away, taking their child with her.

It wasn't just anger and wounded dignity that had made him keep Amber at a distance. The Tris who danced and flirted and seduced wasn't the Tris who worked so tirelessly and endlessly to keep Elsornia healthy and profitable. He barely recognised the man he'd been that night—and that was the man Amber had chosen. Not the workaholic prince who never even took time out to watch a film and couldn't name his favourite song. How could he compete with the fairy tale he'd pretended to be? But how could he not? Not just because he needed Amber to want to stay, but because he needed her. All of her.

Tris pushed away the warning voice reminding him just how badly this could go, pushed away the memories of his mother's unhappiness as his father put duty before their marriage and her needs time and time again. His father had done his best to make him in his image and mostly he'd succeeded, but couldn't Tris do better here? With Amber staring at him, eyes wide, full mouth parted, sweet, beguiling and so beautiful she took his breath away, he had no choice but to try.

Slowly, slowly he sauntered across the floor towards her. Amber made no move to meet him but neither did she retreat. She simply stood stock-still, luminous green eyes fixed on him, her full mouth half parted, her chest rising and falling. Tris stopped still a pace away and held out his hand. There could be no seduction, no coercion, no expectation. No champagne or stars or beguiling words, but a meeting of equals.

Amber didn't move for several long, long seconds and then finally, just as Tris was beginning to wonder if he had imagined the whole connection between them, she took his hand and half stepped a little closer. Neither spoke, fingers entwined as Tris reached out and drew a finger down her cheek, lingering slightly on her lips before skimming down the long column of her neck, finally resting on her shoulder. She barely moved as he touched her, just an almost imperceptible tremble, her eyes half closing. One more step and she was snug against him, her breasts soft against his chest, long firm legs pressed to his, the warmth of her hair on his cheek.

'I've been thinking about kissing you again ever since I woke up the morning after the wedding,' Tris said hoarsely.

'In that case you should go ahead.' Amber smiled up at him as she spoke, her shy yet teasing smile full of promise and anticipation. Heat flooded him. She wanted him, physically at least, and that was far more than he deserved. But only a fool would turn down such an invitation. Slowly, savouring every millisecond, Tris ran his hand along her shoulder, cupping the glorious weight of her hair as he reached the tender skin at the nape of her neck before dipping his head to cover her mouth with his.

Last time they had both been too impatient. The moment they'd kissed had been incendiary, sending them both into a dizzying spiral straight into his bed. Despite the insistent demands of his body, Tris had no intention of taking Amber back to his room tonight. Nor, tempting as it was, was he planning to seduce her in the palace kitchens. This kiss wasn't about seduction but about wooing and so he started slow, nibbling her lower lip, holding her gently as if she were made of porcelain. It was almost more than he could bear, the slow, sweet kiss, harder than anything he'd ever done before as he gently but firmly stopped Amber from speeding things up, holding her lightly, not allowing himself to explore her curves even as she pressed against him. He was playing a long game here, not looking for the easy victory, and so he allowed himself to savour every moment of the kiss, to take in every detail, the fresh floral scent of her hair, her sweet vanilla taste, part-cake part-her, the warmth of her touch, the way her fingers entwined in his, caressing and holding, the softness of her mouth, a mouth made for kissing and being kissed. He needed to savour and remember, imprinting every touch and sensation in his memory.

It was a long time since Tris had believed that his future held anything but duty and responsibility. But standing here, the most beautiful and beguiling woman he'd ever met in his arms, he knew that he had a chance at something more. His future was in her hands. As, he suspected, was his heart.

CHAPTER ELEVEN

AMBER COULD TELL that it was late when she woke the next morning, the angle of the sun slanting into her bedroom a tell-tale clue. She stretched, savouring the sweetness that came from a good night's sleep. It had been late, very late, when she'd finally got to bed. She and Tris had done their best to return the kitchen to the spotless state she'd found it in, hiding every trace of their night-time antics. Baking always made her feel better but for once it wasn't the soothing action of creating that had enabled her to fall into the deep sleep she needed, but those minutes, those wonderful, frustrating, unforgettable moments she'd spent in Tris's arms.

What on earth had happened? One moment she'd been telling Harriet that she had made a terrible mistake, allowing a teenage crush and a night's illusion to give her false hope that she might forge a lasting relationship with Tris, the next she'd found herself confiding in him in a way she'd confided in nobody, not even her friends. Not only that, but he had started to let her in, not all the way, but she understood him a lot more than she had this time yesterday.

And then there were the kisses. Just as intoxicating as she remembered, turning her body limp with desire, her brain to a single-minded entity wanting nothing more than him. She'd yearned for far more than sweet, chaste kisses but this morning she was grateful for Tris's restraint. Their situation was complicated enough without adding sex into it. Of course, some might point out that that particular horse had already bolted but it wasn't the physical consequences of lovemaking that concerned her; it was the emotional ones. Not that she'd been thinking so clearly last night. If the timer hadn't gone off when it had, Amber wasn't sure Tris would have managed to stay so restrained either...

But a proper conversation and a few kisses

didn't solve anything. Yes, she felt a little closer to Tris, but whether that closeness would still exist in the morning light she had yet to find out. One thing she knew: she couldn't leave her future in either Tris's or fate's hands; it was time to take some control of her destiny. No more waiting around for Tris to talk to her or let her in; she was ready to start battering down the drawbridge if that was what she had to do.

Reluctantly, Amber pushed back the sheets and swung her feet to the floor. She wasn't going to solve anything or change anything lying in bed, nor was she going to get where she needed to be living in a luxurious apartment two staircases and three corridors away from Tris, surrounded by servants and aides and soldiers.

Pulling on her robe, she padded upstairs to her turret-top terrace, texting Tris as she did so, rewarded five minutes later when he walked in carrying a tray heaped with fresh fruit, coffee and still warm pastries.

'Good morning,' he said and then looked at the sun. 'Or should I say good afternoon?'

Amber was acutely aware that she was still in her pyjamas and robe, her hair barely brushed, her face make-up-free, although she had managed to clean her teeth. But she wanted intimacy and there was nothing as intimate as breakfast. 'Don't tell me you've been up for hours?'

'Since six,' he said and laughed as she pulled a horrified face.

'That's less than four hours sleep; you'd better sit down and have a pastry. As you may have realised last night, I'm a firm believer that food solves everything, even if you don't make it yourself.'

'Yes, last night was very informative.'

Amber felt her cheeks heat at the unexpectedly teasing tone in Tris's voice. 'I'm glad you thought so.' She managed to keep her own tone light. 'I'm planning a repeat as soon as possible. You made a very creditable cake; more lessons are definitely in order.'

'With a teacher like you, how can I fail to improve?'

Amber was fully aware that Tris wasn't really talking about baking. 'I don't know; it seems to me that you weren't quite as inexperienced as I thought.'

This was definite progress, sitting here in the late spring sunshine enjoying brunch together, the conversation easy yet intimate with a subtext only they understood, but there was still a long way to go. Tris hadn't touched her since he'd arrived, let alone kissed her; there was still a distance between them, physically and mentally. Amber's parents had touched all the time, little caresses and pats, careless kisses dropped on cheeks and foreheads, hands reaching for each other automatically. She hadn't realised as a child how rare that casual intimacy was between married couples; it was something she'd always expected to experience herself one day. Now, even though she knew it was rare, she still yearned for a marriage as complete as her parents' had been.

Maybe it was unfair to expect that kind of relationship from a man who had had a very different kind of childhood. But last night there had been glimpses of another Tris, of the man she had danced and laughed and made love with just a few weeks ago.

She sipped her coffee and summoned up her courage. 'I have a request.'

'Anything.'

'I thought we discussed the folly of making unlimited promises last night. What if I asked for half the kingdom or insisted you only served pink food? Although you might find either of those requests a little easier to agree to.'

'Intriguing.' But Tris looked more wary than intrigued.

'I'd like you to take a vacation. A fortnight somewhere here in Elsornia that you really love. Not the castle, not surrounded by servants and guards and bureaucrats and people needing you every second of the day, but somewhere where we can just be ourselves. Somewhere I don't have to sneak into the kitchen to bake if I don't want to be surrounded by sous chefs trying to anticipate my every need.'

Tris put down his coffee, his forehead

creased. 'Amber, I understand, I really do, but it's not that easy for me to just take time off.'

She held up her hand to forestall the inevitable reasons why. 'I don't mean today. This time next week I'm flying to London for a couple of days to have my twelve-week scan. I don't expect you to come with me; in fact it's easier if you don't, not until we have a better idea of our future. All it needs is one picture leaked to the press of you and me near a maternity unit and our secret is out.'

'That makes sense,' Tris agreed, but he was wearing the shuttered look that frustrated her so much, hiding his real thoughts and emotions from her.

With a deep breath, Amber continued. 'Normally, if this scan is okay, which, fingers crossed it is, I wouldn't need to have another one until about twenty weeks. But if you want I could book a private scan for sixteen weeks. That's a good time to find out the sex of the baby with some accuracy. I do understand how important having a son is to you. If the baby is a girl...'

'If the baby is a girl I still want to marry

you.' Tris's jaw was set, his grey eyes dark with an emotion she couldn't identify. She tightened her hold on her cup, wishing the coffee had the kick of caffeine she needed to help sharpen her mind. Did he mean that? Or was he saying what he thought she wanted to hear? But through the doubt there was a tinge of relief—she would rather wait to find out the sex of the baby. She'd always imagined having a family of her own and, so far, none of this pregnancy had borne any resemblance to those dreams. It would be lovely to keep an element of surprise and anticipation, no matter what happened.

Choosing her words carefully, she looked over at him. 'I appreciate you saying that, I really do, but surely if we know the baby's a girl it would simplify things somewhat? I know co-parenting without marriage will be tricky for you, with the eyes of the world on you the way they are. And I'm fully aware of how difficult life will be for the illegitimate daughter of the King, if her parentage was known. But it would be just as difficult if she was brought up with parents who marry for the wrong reasons. I'm not willing to sacrifice all our happiness for a throne, Tris. I know your parents weren't happy; surely you don't want to repeat that history with your own children?'

'I promise to do all that is in my power to make you happy,' Tris said stiffly and Amber raised her hand and laid it upon his cheek.

'I know, and I also know that I can't rely on you or anyone for my happiness, that I have to take responsibility for myself. But marriage does need two people's focus to make it work, even ones with a much more auspicious start than ours, and my worry is how much of that focus will be actually in your power and how much you will sacrifice to duty. How much *we* will have to sacrifice to duty. So please, when I get back from London, let's spend time alone, just the two of us, and decide if this is something that we can both not just live with, but *want* to live with.'

Tris reached up and covered her hand with his. 'Let me see what I can do; maybe two weeks isn't impossible if I move some things around.'

Amber squeezed his hand in relief. 'Thank you, Tris. I know I'm not the only one trying to work out the right thing to do here. I do appreciate everything you're trying to do, I really do.' She turned her hand and threaded her fingers through his, his clasp warm and strong and comforting.

Amber had no doubt that Tris would try his hardest to be supportive and to make her feel that she belonged in his world. She also suspected that he was beginning to care for her, Amber Blakeley, not just the mother of his unborn baby. But was that enough? Once they were safely married, once the baby was here, would duty dominate his life as it had done in the past, leaving her just a few scraps of his attention? Amber didn't need a man to dance attendance on her all the time, but neither did she want the kind of marriage where she felt she'd be better off alone. She'd seen what was possible in a partnership of equals; could she really settle for less? But sitting here, her hand in Tris's, the sun warm upon her face, she had hope for the first time in months that things might just work out the way she hoped.

Tris stood in the small private courtyard and watched the car containing Amber, and with her all his hopes, disappear out of the discreet side entrance. In less than an hour she would be on a private flight back to London, not returning for a couple of days. If at all. There was nothing compelling her to come back, just her promise.

'You should have gone with her,' Elisabetta said softly, coming to stand beside him. 'That's your baby too. Or she could have had the scan here.' Tris had finally, with Amber's permission, told his sister about the pregnancy the day before, upon the promise of the utmost secrecy. She'd been delighted, if more than a little confused. No wonder when she'd seen the awkwardness between them, the constrained silences as they sought to understand the other better, although the week since his bakery lesson—and the kisses they had shared—had been different. There had been no repeat of the kisses or of the lesson, but there had been an ease which was as welcome as it was new.

'There's no way we could keep the pregnancy private if she had the scan here, you know that. And she wanted to be in London, with her friends. They mean a lot to her, they're her family.' Tris completely understood Amber's reasoning, the common sense part of him agreed with her, but there was another part of him that wished she wanted him there; he couldn't imagine how it would feel to see a glimpse of the baby for the first time, for them to experience that moment together.

Elisabetta shot him a quick glance. 'You're her family too. No matter what happens next, being parents will bind you.'

'Like it bound our parents?' Tris said more bitterly than he meant to, and his sister looped her arm through his.

'No, because you are better than that. Our father failed when he tried to turn you into a carbon copy of him, thank goodness, and Amber has more optimism, more independence than Mama ever did. She'll find her path no matter what—her life so far is proof of that. Leaving New York with less than a thousand dollars in her pocket at just eighteen to start a new life in a new country? That takes a lot of grit, Tris.'

'She should never have had to leave like that. I should never have agreed to our uncle's proposal. But I knew it was what Father would have wanted. Pathetic, isn't it, trying to make a dead man happy? Especially as I never really managed it when he was alive.'

'He was proud of you, Tris, I genuinely believe that; he just had no idea how to show it. You were a good son, just like you are a good brother and I know you will be a wonderful father.'

Tris didn't answer, his eyes still fixed on the spot where the car had disappeared. *A father.* It was strange, but he hadn't really thought about what that meant before. Oh, he had thought about the throne and cementing his position as King, thought about marriage to the woman who had eluded him for so long, but not about the reality of what being a father meant. Not about an actual baby who would need to be cared for, held and rocked and changed and fed. A small child who would need to be played with and taught right from wrong. An older child with opinions and likes different to his own. A combination of Amber and him, maybe with her hair and his eyes, her smile and exuberant sweetness or his diffidence and reserve. Excitement and panic filled him in equal measure. There was so much at stake, so much scope to get things wrong. How did anyone feel fit to embark on parenthood, with all its mishaps and pitfalls?

'How do you know that?' He turned to face his sister. 'What if I get it wrong? I'm too strict? Always too busy? Expect too much? Show my disappointment?'

What if he or she doesn't love me?

He couldn't say the last words but Elisabetta must have sensed them because she wrapped her arms around him in a brief hug before stepping back with a warm smile.

'The very fact you are asking these questions shows what a wonderful father you'll be. I bet our father never once doubted himself, never once wondered if he was making a mistake. Keep wondering, Tris, keep questioning, keep listening—and, most importantly, keep loving and you will do just fine.'

Keep loving.

It sounded so easy, but Tris knew how hard that could be—and knew how dark the consequences of a loveless childhood could be. Things would be different, he vowed. Whatever Amber decided, he would love their baby, make sure it knew how much it was wanted, how special it was. No matter what.

CHAPTER TWELVE

TRIS'S HANDS TIGHTENED on the steering wheel as he navigated his car around a tight bend. On one side a sheer wall of rock rose dizzyingly into the heights above them, on the other an even more sheer drop fell straight into the valley below. This drive was not for the faint-hearted, but Amber didn't seem afraid; she'd wound the window down and the wind ruffled her hair as she looked out at the countryside spread before her.

This was the wilder, more remote side of Elsornia, an area where few foreign tourists ventured, where villages were few and far between and sheep and goats outnumbered people. Down in the valley the forests spread as far as the eye could see, although Tris knew that another bend in the road would reveal the lake that was their destination.

It was years since he'd last driven along this road, years since he'd been to the villa his mother had retreated to as her marriage broke down, to raise his sisters. He knew the price of that separation was leaving him behind; knowing he'd have chosen to stay didn't make the pain of that choice any easier to forget.

His grip tightened further. Not for the first time, he questioned his decision to bring Amber to the place which provoked such conflicting feelings in him. But he'd prevaricated enough. Amber needed to know more of him, and the villa by the lake was the only place he had ever allowed himself to feel free. As soon as she'd asked him to take her somewhere special, he'd known this was the only possible destination.

Tris glanced quickly at Amber as she leaned into the breeze, her gaze still fixed on the distant horizon. 'You're sure you're not queasy?'

Despite his attempt to remain nonchalant, a thrill ran through him as he awaited her answer. She looked exactly the same, not an ounce heavier yet, but everything had changed nonetheless. She'd barely greeted him at the private airfield before she handed him a small, fuzzy black and white photo of something that looked like a cross between an alien and a tadpole. Their baby. Staring down at the indistinct image, Tris had experienced emotion like he'd never felt before, pure, overwhelming and all-encompassing, a knowledge that he'd do anything, sacrifice everything to keep this tiny, vulnerable hope and the woman who bore it safe.

'I'm fine,' Amber said, leaning back in her seat. 'I'm officially past the first three months now so hopefully I've avoided all queasiness. Apparently this is when I get lots of energy.'

Tris couldn't stop the wry smile curling his mouth. 'So the last few weeks you've been lacking in energy? Was that when you insisted on learning that country dance at the school, or was it when you walked up to the glacier and refused the lift back down? You *did* look weary when we finally finished washing up after your mammoth baking session, but you are the one who thought eleven p.m. was a good time to start making cakes.'

'Any time is a good time for baking,' Amber said with dignity. 'Have I taught you nothing?'

Tris didn't reply, the next hairpin bend needing all his concentration, but despite the difficult roads he was aware that for the first time in a really long time he was actually relaxed. More than that, he was happy. Waiting at the airfield, he'd been fully prepared for the news that Amber had changed her mind, that she'd decided to stay in London and continue her pregnancy there. But it hadn't just been relief he'd felt when he saw her disembark from the plane; it had been joy. Not because of the child she carried, but because she'd returned. Returned to give him a second chance. He couldn't—mustn't—blow it.

He'd missed her while she'd been away. Missed the way she hummed as she busied herself, her bright, cheery conversation. Missed the way she drew him out, until he found himself opening up, surprising himself. Somehow, over the last two weeks, she'd got under his skin. Tris had no idea what that meant for their future, but he knew he had to do his utmost to make sure the next two weeks were everything she needed to make a decision to stay.

'Do you mind if I put some music on?' Without waiting for his assent, Amber pulled out her phone and connected it to the car's Bluetooth. 'I'd ask you what you wanted, but after the other night I realised that you need a little bit of educating. A lot of educating if I want to be brutally honest rather than diplomatic. Baking obviously, films absolutely, books without a doubt and, most importantly of all, music. Music is good for the soul whether it's classical, pop, reggae or R&B, so I put together a playlist. It's a little eclectic, but I wanted to cover as many bases as possible. Okay, your education starts here…'

The sound of a piano filled the car, soon joined by a soaring soprano voice, followed by a thumping dance track and then an upbeat musical number. Amber hadn't been kidding when she said her playlist was eclectic, but Tris didn't care what the music was. He was just absurdly touched that in the short time she'd been away she'd spent thought and effort putting together a playlist just for him.

In no time at all they started the descent down the mountain to the huge lake which made this part of Elsornia a popular holiday destination. One or two villages turned into fashionable resorts during the summer months, with swimming areas and plentiful berths for boats along the shoreline, but most of it remained unspoilt.

When Tris was small, the lake had been the royal family's favourite summer vacation spot, but after his mother moved permanently to their holiday home his father stayed away, allowing Tris just a month there every summer. He'd worked hard not to envy his sisters growing up in the relative freedom of the countryside, away from castle politics and the prying eyes of the media, spending their term times at boarding school and the holidays with their mother, but there had been times when the contrast between their carefree childhood and his own was too stark and he hadn't returned here since his mother had left, ten years before.

'This is absolutely gorgeous.' Amber stared out of the window like a child looking for the sea. 'The lake is so blue. I don't think I've ever seen water that colour before.'

'Legend says it's so blue because when Hera found out about Zeus's affair with Europa she flew off in anger until she reached this valley. The trees sheltered her from the other gods' view and so she allowed her tears of humiliation and rage and sadness to flow. Of course, Zeus was known for his affairs and there were a lot of tears when she started to shed them. So many that she flooded half the valley with her melancholy.'

'I can't decide if that's a beautiful tale or just a really sad one,' Amber said. 'I suppose creating a lake was a better thing to do than torturing some poor girl who had no choice once Zeus had decided to turn into a ball or a swan or shower of gold, whatever shenanigans he decided upon that time. I always thought it really unfair that the goddesses went around punishing the poor women when it was the gods who did the preying.'

'You know your mythology.'

'I can thank my dad for that; he loved Greek myths. He used to read them to me every night. The children's version at first, then his favourite translations of Ovid, the *Iliad*, the *Odyssey*. We were about to move on to the *Aeneid* when he died. I've still never read it; I didn't have the heart somehow. Maybe one day I'll read it to our baby.' Her voice was wistful, and she blinked a couple of times before turning back to look out of the window.

Tris wanted to say something comforting, something wise, but couldn't find the words so he drove instead, after a while humming along a little to the music until Amber laughed at his attempts to follow the tune. In no time at all they were on the lakeside road leading to the villa. It was all so achingly familiar. Trees lined the road on one side, the lake glinted in the late spring sun on the other. A few boats bobbed up and down on the water, birds circling overhead, occasionally diving into the blue depths and emerging triumphantly, something silver glittering in their beaks.

Amber was transfixed. 'Can you swim in the lake?'

'You can, but it's fed from the mountains so only the hardiest souls venture in before the summer. And it's never exactly warm even then, but the outside temperature can get so hot that no one cares.'

'I love to wild swim,' Amber said dreamily. 'Sometimes in London I go to the pond on Hampstead Heath or the Serpentine Lido but it's not the same as really wild swimming. I'd like to come back here when it's warm enough.' Her words warmed him. In spite of the memories the lake held, maybe because of them, Tris had known it was the right place to bring her. The right place to see if the liking and understanding so slowly growing between them could become something more permanent.

They drove on through several villages, the first two full of second homes owned by wealthy Elsornian families, filled with fashionable restaurants and bistros and plenty of expensive shops. The next village along was less well-to-do but a great deal more charming with its neighbourhood cafés and small *tavernas*. Amber exclaimed in delight as they passed through it, proclaiming her intention to return and sample cakes from the bakery on the high street. As they drove out, the road began to snake away from the lakeside, skirting round a tall metal fence. A few hundred yards later Tris turned in at a pair of huge iron gates which swung open at his approach.

'I know you asked for us to spend time alone,' he said as he eased the car along the driveway. 'I can't quite give you that, but I can promise you no officials or secretaries or aides. We employ several local people here—gardeners, maids, people to look after the villa—but they live out. There will always be a handful of bodyguards around, I couldn't lose those if I tried, but they're trained to be discreet. You shouldn't even notice they are here.'

'Thank you,' Amber said. She touched his arm, the ease of the gesture warming him through. 'I really appreciate all the effort you've gone to.'

Just a few moments later they were inside

the pretty white villa. It was a complete contrast to the thick-walled stone medieval castle where Tris had been brought up and now lived. Built on graceful Italianate lines, the rooms were light-filled and airy, tiled floors and high ceilings offering respite from the hot summers, whilst large stoves in every room ensured warmth in the brief but cold winter months. Elegantly furnished in shades of blue, it was an inviting space, enhanced by breathtaking views from the floor-to-ceiling windows which ran along the whole back wall of the house, looking out onto the lake.

'Privacy glass and bullet-proof,' Tris informed Amber as she exclaimed in delight. 'The royal guard had a fit when we first started coming here; they said that anyone could just zoom in from the lake.'

'They have a point, I suppose.' Amber stared out at the lake. 'Is it likely?'

'I doubt it. A large area of the lake is a no-go zone and anyone who enters it is immediately accosted. Guards are stationed at checkpoints whenever the family is resident and there's a panic room in the basement, so don't worry. The truth is Elsornia has always been fairly stable; even at the end of the nineteenth century when most small kingdoms were hotbeds of revolutionaries, we only had a few half-hearted attempts. From what I can tell, our firebrands were more interested in cryptic passwords and hosting meetings than actually overthrowing the government. We managed to ride out the period between the Wars and post-war turbulence with nothing more than some fiery speeches and the odd badly attended parade.'

'I don't know much about when my family left Belravia,' Amber said, turning away from the window and walking over to look at a landscape on the wall, 'but it must have been terrifying. My grandfather was only a tiny baby and he had to be smuggled out—they would have shot him if they'd found him. I've never understood why he was so keen to go back after that experience.'

'If he hadn't left then he would have had to go when the Soviets moved in. All that area became part of the Soviet Union. I think your father was very sensible, moving on the way he did.'

'Wise and more than a little relieved. He hated bureaucracy and meetings. I think he'd have been a terrible king, found it all too tedious.' She looked at him curiously. 'Are you ever bored?'

The obvious automatic reply was a quick negative. Of course he wasn't bored. How could he be? After all, it was a huge privilege to serve his country; his father had impressed that on him every day. But sometimes, sitting in yet another long meeting or budget discussion or on yet another formal visit, Tris had been aware that something was missing. Over the last few weeks he had started to realise just what that something might be: companionship, laughter, maybe even love. 'It's not something I let myself think about,' he said honestly.

'Everyone should be bored sometimes; Dad always said that learning to cope with it builds character. But I promise there will be no character-building in that way this holiday; I have too much educating to do. I hope you got the shopping list I sent you?'

'Kitchen fully stocked, ma'am.' He saluted her and his heart lifted as Amber let out a peal of laughter. It couldn't be this easy, this simple, spending time together. Could it?

'Come on then, show me around,' she said, taking his arm. 'I want every detail of every scrape you got into when you were young. No matter how embarrassing.'

'I'll do my best but, I warn you, my childhood was about as exciting as my adult life so don't expect too much.'

Amber raised her eyebrows. 'I don't know; you managed to get a stranger pregnant from a one-night stand and then found out you were engaged to her all along. That doesn't sound boring to me.'

'No,' he agreed. 'Things have definitely livened up recently.'

Amber kept her hand tucked into his arm as Tris showed her around the villa. Imposing as it was, it was still a family home, not a political seat like the castle, and the tour didn't take too long, even with Amber stopping to admire the view from every single room.

'I've put you in what used to be my mother's room,' Tris said, opening the door into a charming suite of rooms overlooking the lake, a balcony leading from the dressing room.

Amber stopped and looked at him anxiously. 'Won't she mind?'

'Oh, no. She lives in Switzerland now, with her second husband; she never comes back here.'

'That seems so sad when she lived here for such a long time. Why doesn't she come back?'

Tris stepped over to the window. How many times had his mother looked out at the lake and the mountains beyond, feeling trapped and helpless? 'She feels that she was exiled here.'

'Oh?'

Tris had known that visiting the villa again meant laying some ghosts, even if not all the spirits were dead. He tried to keep his voice neutral. 'What do you know about my parents?'

Amber glanced at him quickly. 'Not much. I mean I know your father died when you were about twenty, but I don't think my grandmother ever really mentioned your mother. Nor have you. There're no pictures of her anywhere.'

'No, my father gradually removed them all. He was an unforgiving man and she hurt his pride, if not his heart.'

'I'm sorry, I didn't mean to pry. You don't have to tell me anything else if you don't want to.'

Amber might have meant every word, but Tris knew that this holiday was crucial in her decision whether to stay in Elsornia with him or return home, and that his inability to open up was weighing against him. 'Do you want some air?' he asked and, without waiting for an answer, unlocked the door to the balcony and stepped outside. How many times had he found his mother out here, a forbidden cigarette in one hand, a black coffee in the other as she stared bleakly at the mountains which cut her off from the parties and company she craved. Only in the summer, when the villages were filled with visitors, did she come alive. He knew without looking that Amber had joined him, leaning on the wooden balcony by his side.

'My mother, like you, came from a dispossessed royal house, which is why my father considered her a suitable bride. Also, like you, a life full of pomp and duty wasn't really what she wanted. Oh, she tried, but my father was a very austere and conscientious man. Elsornia always came first and she really struggled with that, with him. When I was ten, she and my sisters moved here. They told everyone it was temporary, for her health, but the reality was she left my father, and she left me with him.'

'Oh, Tris, that must have been so hard for you.'

His throat dried; the sympathy in her voice was almost more than he could bear.

'My father refused to grant her a divorce. Instead he gave her an ultimatum: live here with her daughters, stay at the castle with us all or leave alone. She chose the girls. She left the villa the week after my father's funeral; less than a year later she remarried.'

'Did you see much of her? Of your sisters?'

'A few weeks in the summer, that was all. My father didn't have much time for my sisters. Girls were no use to him; they couldn't inherit and marrying them off wasn't really an option in the twenty-first century. His loss. My sisters are lovely, warm women and they are also scarily brilliant. As you know, Elisabetta works with me, she speaks four languages fluently and has a PhD in International Relations. Giuliana is a trained pilot and is a shining light in the Air Force and Talia is still at university, doing something with physics I quite frankly don't understand.'

'They sound most formidable; if I didn't already know Elisabetta I'd be terrified of them.' Amber moved closer, placing a soft hand on his shoulder. 'It sounds like your mother had to make some very difficult choices. I'm sure she loves you.'

'It was a long time ago. I don't really think

about it any more.' The lie hung there as he turned away and the pressure increased on his shoulder, her other arm sliding around his waist as she pressed herself against his back, all softness and warmth and understanding. It was almost more than he could bear.

'You don't have to pretend with me, Tris. You never have to pretend with me.'

Tris wanted to tell her that he wasn't pretending, that he'd been fine then and he was definitely fine now. That his father had been right, Tris had needed to grow up and start being responsible, not spend his days larking around on the lake and wasting his time playing with his sisters and cousins. But the words wouldn't come. Instead he turned, gathering her into his arms, burying his head into her hair, holding her close.

Her understanding, her comfort was dangerous, but he couldn't step away. He didn't want to need her; he didn't want to need anyone. Need led to betrayal and disappointment; he'd learned that lesson young and never forgotten it. The formal agreement he'd signed with Amber's grandmother, the formal arrangement he'd assumed they'd come to in the lawyer's office in Paris had suited him fine: a wife, an heir, his life neatly tied up with no emotional mess. How could he have believed that future possible when he knew how she felt, how she tasted, how her warmth enveloped him until the chill deep in his bones disappeared? There was nothing neat or tidy about Amber and the way she made him feel. And that made him so, so vulnerable.

Right now Tris couldn't help but accept the comfort she offered, tilting her chin, searching her gaze with his for consent before taking her mouth in a deep claiming kiss that branded her on his heart. This was no seduction, no tease, no sweet playfulness but deep and raw and almost painful.

Amber didn't pull back. Instead she pressed closer, entwining her arms around him, kissing him back fiercely as if trying to prove that he was worth something after all. How he wished he could believe it, could believe in himself as much as he believed in her.

* * *

Amber stretched out on the sofa and waved her book at Tris. 'Look what Harriet gave me. Us,' she corrected herself.

'What is it?'

'Baby names. You don't have one of those lists that royal children have to be named from, do you? As someone saddled with Vasilisa as my middle name, I have strong feelings about names.'

'No, no lists.' Tris perched on the arm next to her and Amber leaned her head against his leg, enjoying the intimacy. They'd been at the villa for a couple of days now and every moment felt easier and easier, as if they were together by choice, not circumstance. Tris seemed younger, lighter, away from the castle and the all-consuming summons of his phones and aides, and in return Amber felt herself drawn more and more to him.

Theirs was a slow courtship, a contrast to the way they'd met, when they'd rushed into intimacy with such life-changing consequences. Instead they held hands as Tris showed her his favourite lakeside walk and indulged in long, sweet, slow kissing sessions that left Amber breathless with desire. If this was being wooed then she liked it, this anticipation of touch, this easy communication. It was everything she had always hoped for in a relationship. She couldn't believe this was Tris, the uptight, upright, closed-off prince, jeans-clad and relaxed beside her.

'In that case, do you have any favourites?' Amber was aware she held all the cards in this pregnancy; it was her decision whether they married, whether she stayed in Elsornia, whether Tris was a full-time father or an occasional parent. She wanted the name to mean something to him. As long as he didn't saddle the baby with something as hard to live with as Vasilisa, that was.

Tris took the book from her and leafed through the pages. 'You've been busy underlining,' he said, one hand resting casually on her hair. 'Artemis, Athene, Hector? I sense a theme.'

'My dad really wanted to call me Athene, but my mother said no way—but if the baby has your eyes then it would be fitting, don't you think? Grey-eyed Athene?'

'I don't know; naming a baby after a goddess seems to give it an awful lot to live up to. What was your mother's name?'

'Rosemary. My dad was Svetoslav, but he changed it to Stephen when he moved to the UK.'

'Okay then, Rosa or Stefano. How does that sound?'

Amber sat up, turning to Tris in surprise. 'Really?'

'If it would make you happy.'

She blinked, her throat tight. 'If it would make me happy? I can't think of anything that would make me happier. I've been missing them so much recently. I don't know if it's talking about them with you, or realising I'm going to have this baby without my mother to help me.' She tried to summon a smile but could feel it wobbling. 'I know it's silly, I've had to do so much without her, but I really wish she was here. She would have been such a great grandmother.'

'She'll be with you,' Tris said, cupping her

cheek softly. 'Every time you bake with our daughter or son your mother will be there, every myth you read our child your dad will be reading along with you.'

For a moment all she could do was stare wordlessly at him as his words sunk in, each one warming her soul. 'You're right. As long as I keep our traditions alive, as long as they're in my heart they're here. Thank you, Tris.' She leaned in and kissed him, a brief, sweet caress. 'And thank you for the names. It's the most beautiful gesture; I'll never forget it. Never forget that you brought me here to this beautiful place...'

'Amber. It's the least I can do. You're not just giving me a baby; you're giving me a chance to prove myself to you. I know what it's cost you. I just want you to know that I appreciate it.'

'Right now, you're making it very easy...' She didn't know who kissed who this time, the kiss lengthening as she lost herself in him, Tris shifting until Amber was pressed close, her arms entwined around his neck, his hand on her back, warming her through as her body trembled with want, needing him closer, not wanting any barriers between them.

'Tris?' She pulled back, looking him full in the face, letting him see her desire and need, letting everything she felt show in her eyes, in her parted mouth, her ragged breath. 'I want you, all of you. Make love to me, Tris, please.'

He was almost preternaturally still, only his eyes alive, scorching as he stared at her, his gaze moving slowly to her mouth, to the exposed skin at her neck where her pulse beat frantically, to her chest. Slowly, oh, so slowly, he moved it back up to meet her gaze. 'Are you sure?'

'I've never been surer of anything in my life.' And she hadn't. This wasn't the combined magic of moonlight, champagne and a long dormant crush; this was the knowledge that the man beside her would never intentionally hurt her, was beginning to know her heart, and that was far more intoxicating than any romantic evening. 'I want you, Tris.'

Finally, his mouth curved into a wolfish smile and she shivered at the heat in his eyes. 'In that case, my lady, how can I refuse?'

CHAPTER THIRTEEN

'WHAT DO YOU want to do today?' Amber leaned back against the pillows and watched Tris dress with unashamed appreciation. He had far too good a body for a prince who claimed to spend most of his time in meetings; those lean muscles didn't come from a gym but from a man who loved the outdoors and knew how to handle himself in it. She wriggled with contentment as she shifted. It wasn't the only thing he knew how to handle…

They'd been at the villa for nearly two weeks now and Tris had spent every night, since the afternoon they'd started to pick baby names and ended up making love, in her bed. She loved waking up with his arm wrapped around her waist, the warmth and heaviness of him next to her. He made her feel safe.

Wanted. Needed—and not just because of the baby she carried. And it wasn't all one-sided. She valued his opinions, his thoughtfulness and good sense, just as she enjoyed watching him relax more and more each day. Amber wasn't entirely sure what she'd expected from their holiday, but it certainly wasn't this contented ease and intimacy.

Sliding her hand down to caress the slight curve of her belly, she sat up a little more, all the better to watch him dress. 'We made good progress on the films yesterday, although how you fell asleep during my favourite dance movie I do not know. Definitely several marks lost there.'

'No films today.' Tris pulled a T-shirt over his head.

Amber approved of this more casual Tris. His hair was a little messy and he had even allowed a hint of stubble to appear, giving him an edgy sexiness. She especially liked knowing that this relaxed part of him was kept secret from nearly everybody, that it was hers alone.

'Not even one film?'

They'd quickly fallen into a pattern. If the weather was good they went out for a walk or a sail on the lake, coming back mid-afternoon to either watch one of the films from the list Amber had put together or to read in companionable silence. Whilst in London she'd bought an e-reader and filled it with a selection of her favourite books for him.

'You have to start at the beginning,' she'd explained to Tris, so she'd included some of her own coming-of-age favourites and if they weren't exactly Tris's preferred reading he hadn't said so. Like the playlists of songs and the list of movies, she'd tried to put together a real mix to allow him to discover his own preferences—although if that preference didn't include *Dirty Dancing* she had a lot more educating to do.

On cooler or wet days they either explored the charming villages and towns along the lakeside or carried on with baking lessons. The quiet, tranquil days suited her perfectly. The pregnancy and its ramifications had rocked her more than she'd realised; it wasn't until she had her scan that she really understood just how much her life was going to change. She also knew she really didn't want to raise a baby alone if she didn't have to, that she was going to do everything in her power to make a relationship with Tris work.

She just hadn't expected spending time with him to be so easy, to make the thought of extending her stay, even making a life here actually enticing not just bearable. Gone was the austere, closed-off Prince from the castle; instead Tris was proving to be a really entertaining companion. An entertaining companion and a good lover. More, she was beginning to see beneath the surface, beginning to understand how his father's demands and his mother's desertion had shaped him. Every time he let her in she felt herself fall a little more.

If only this holiday could go on for ever, but all too soon they would return to real life and then she'd discover if this was just a holiday romance and all the steps they'd made would be wiped away by the tide of reality.

It was scary how much she hoped for the

former, even as she prepared herself for the latter.

Tris crossed the room and sat down beside her, taking her hand in his, his grip firm and tender. 'I hope you don't mind, but when my sisters heard we were here they went on a big nostalgia trip. To be fair, it was their home for a decade; Talia was only four when she moved here. Somehow they seem to have invited themselves for the weekend. I only realised they actually meant it and are on their way this morning when I checked the family group chat. I know you wanted to be alone...'

'I did, but your sisters are different. Of course I'd like to spend some more time with Elisabetta and meet your other sisters. What do they know about me? About us?'

'Elisabetta knows everything, of course, but the other two know nothing more than when you came: that we met at the wedding and I somehow persuaded you to spend some time here before making up your mind whether to cancel the betrothal agreement or not. I have to warn you that Talia thinks it's all very romantic. In her head the betrothal and your disappearance has made you into some kind of fairy tale heroine. Giuliana, on the other hand, thinks you did exactly the right thing to run away and can't understand what on earth made you come back.'

Interesting—that was pretty much how she'd felt, torn between knowing that life wasn't so easy and neat, that a happy-ever-after was more of a dream than a reality, and the romantic fantasies of her lonely teens. Fantasies that felt more and more real with Tris next to her, lean and strong and still absurdly handsome. But now there was a third way, not so all or nothing, a way of compromise and learning and understanding and, yes, affection and liking at the very least. Maybe even more one day, if the happiness of the last couple of weeks didn't evaporate when they returned to the castle. And guests, even welcome ones, signalled the start of that reality seeping into their idyll.

'Your other sisters don't know about the baby?'

'No. I didn't want to tell them until I knew what your decision was. Although, Amber, even if you decide not to stay, they have a right to know...'

'Of course they do!' Amber interrupted him. 'Both my parents were only children and I'm an only child too. I can give this baby the best three honorary aunts in the world, but how amazing for it to have three actual aunts as well.'

She pushed back the covers, optimism filling her. Staying in Elsornia and marrying Tris wouldn't be easy, she knew that. She'd have to give up her job, live far away from her friends and her life would be under the kind of scrutiny she'd always avoided. But hadn't she been bemoaning the fact that the agency was changing? Weren't her friends moving on to start lives of their own away from the Chelsea townhouse? And although she would have to endure some media scrutiny, Elsornia was a small country with little international influence. Her position would be very similar to Emilia's, and so far she and Laurent seemed to be avoiding too much press speculation. Maybe this would, could, work out after all.

She smiled over at Tris. 'What time are they getting here?'

'About lunchtime. I thought we might pop into the village to stock up. Talia loves the little cakes from the bakery there and Giuliana has been emailing me demanding a specific kind of bread she claims only they make. What do you think about barbecuing tonight? The evenings have been so warm, and I think the girls would enjoy it.'

The optimism deepened. A life with Tris wouldn't be all pomp and circumstance; their child's life needn't be too unconventional. There was still space to live like this, with no servants, to discuss casually popping into the village to buy food for weekend visitors.

'After lunch?' Amber sauntered over to him and entwined her arms around his neck. 'In that case, there's no need to rush. Why don't you come back to bed for a while…?'

Several hours later, she was a little more nervous. After they'd eventually got up, they'd wandered along the lakeside path into the village to stock up on enough food for an entire week of guests, not just a twenty-four-hour visit. Amber loved how little notice the villagers took of Tris and her. They were treated just like any other citizens, with a disinterested friendliness that disarmed her. Afterwards she'd rushed around tidying the villa and making sure that Tris's sisters' bedrooms, still decorated for the teenagers they had been when they'd left, were aired and made up. Tris had suggested asking one of the live out maids who cleaned the villa to come and help, but Amber had wanted to hold on to the sweet normality a little longer. There was something endearing about Tris's complete lack of household skill and he was more of a hindrance than a help as she made up the beds and arranged the flowers she'd bought in the village in each of the rooms. She was aware that this was their home not hers and it was a fine line between making their rooms welcoming and stamping her mark on their childhood home.

'Don't worry, they're going to love you,' Tris reassured her, and Amber leaned into him gratefully.

'I always wanted sisters,' she told him

wistfully. 'Maybe it's the books I read. *Little Women, Ballet Shoes*—all those school stories my mother passed on to me, but it always seemed that even when you weren't getting on, sisters were a team. Maybe that's the rose-coloured view of an only child, but I do want to make a good impression on yours.'

She was still patting the last cushion into place when the buzzer indicated that a car was approaching the gate. The invisible guards responded and by the time Tris had opened the front door Amber could see two cars proceeding down the driveway.

'That's odd,' Tris said. 'I wonder why they brought two cars.'

'Maybe they want to leave at different times?' Amber suggested, taking a step closer to Tris, relieved as he clasped her hand in his.

'Maybe. But both Elisabetta and Talia hate the mountain roads; Giuliana is designated driver.' His grip tightened and apprehension crept over her as a cloud covered the warm spring sun. The first car drew up by the side of the house, the second parking next to it and within ten seconds Amber was enveloped in hugs and kisses as Elisabetta and her sisters swooped upon her.

'It's so lovely to see you again—you look really well; the lake air suits you.'

'At last! I've been so excited to meet you. I hope Tris is looking after you properly; he is not half as stuffy as he seems, you know.'

'I can't believe my brother has actually persuaded you to give him a chance; you'll have to tell me how he did it. Tris has many redeeming qualities, but charm is not one of them!'

It was almost overwhelming, but the friendly greetings were a balm to Amber's soul. To be able to give her baby a warm, loving family like this was more than she had ever hoped for, but alongside the relief her heart ached for Tris, raised so differently to his sisters. How different would he have been if his mother had been able to raise him too? But she knew it wasn't too late for him; the last weeks had shown that.

Amber looked around for him, hoping that he'd see how happy this visit was making her, only to realise that he stood stock-still, staring at the occupants of the second car. A tall man, holding the hand of a little girl aged around three, stood next to it, making no move to join their group.

'Nikolai? I didn't know we were going to have the pleasure of your company as well.' It was as if they were back in Paris, Tris's voice was so cold and emotionless.

'Tris.' Nikolai nodded in greeting. 'I bumped into Giuliana yesterday and when she said she was coming here I invited myself along. I hope you don't mind, but I was intrigued to meet your mystery guest.'

'Of course, we are delighted to have you. Amber, this is my cousin Nikolai, and his daughter Isabella. Nikolai, I would like to introduce you to Her Royal Highness Princess Vasilisa of Belravia.'

A chill stole over her, just as much at the formality in his voice as the use of her hated name and title. Somehow Amber summoned up a welcoming smile and held out a hand to Tris's cousin as he sauntered slowly over to them, his daughter still holding his hand tightly. 'It's a pleasure to meet you, and I'm very excited to meet you, Isabella. I know for a fact that we have some delicious cakes in the house; would you like to come and see?'

At the small girl's delighted acceptance, Amber took the proffered hand and, along with Tris's sisters, took Isabella into the house, leaving the two men standing staring at each other. It was no secret that Nikolai's position as next in line to the throne was behind Tris's need to marry and consolidate his role as not just Crown Prince but King, and as far as she knew the antipathy Tris so clearly felt for his cousin was reciprocated, but she had no idea why Nikolai had decided to visit them today.

But what she did know was that their idyllic escape was over and real life had resumed once again. Was the new, fragile tenderness she and Tris had discovered here at the villa strong enough to weather a return to real life or had it all been an illusion? And what did she want? A life here or to return to London? She still had no idea, but she did know that time was running out. She had to make a decision, and soon.

CHAPTER FOURTEEN

'WHY ARE YOU HERE?' With Nikolai's daughter out of earshot, Tris no longer needed to be civil.

His cousin raised an eyebrow. 'Marcel has a cold and my wife has been kept busy caring for him. My poor Isabella is bored with being confined indoors; I thought she might enjoy a trip to the lake.'

'Quit playing games, Nikolai.' Why did it always have to be this way? It would have been easier in the olden days when a duel was a respectable way to solve conflict.

'What do you think I'm going to do, Tris? Break into the villa and kidnap your beautiful Princess? You think I'm that desperate for the throne?'

Tris's jaw tightened. 'This is how it's going to be: go into the villa, make your excuses, collect your daughter and leave. There are plenty of places you can entertain her, places where I am not.'

For a moment Tris saw something flicker across Nikolai's face, something that looked a little like hurt, before the expression was wiped away as if it had never been.

'I came here because I have something to say to you, and it's in your best interest to listen. Take a boat out with me, Tris? Like old times?'

The request struck a chord. He and Nikolai had been at odds for so long, it was easy to forget the time when they had been close friends, boy adventurers escaping from the castle through the tunnels whenever they could. When did that change? When had his childhood companion become his enemy?

'Half an hour,' he said curtly.

Neither spoke as they made their way to the small dinghy moored on the villa's jetty. Nikolai started the engine as Tris cast off and his cousin expertly steered the boat away from the shore, just like they had all those years ago, both falling back into half remembered roles. Nostalgia and something like regret bit hard as Nikolai coiled the rope: regret for the closeness and companionship he had lost and never replaced.

After they'd travelled a few hundred metres Nikolai slowed down, killing the engine as he turned to face his cousin. 'Remember that time we went fishing at midnight? Your father was furious when they caught us. But then it didn't take much to make him furious, did it?'

'That's what you came here for? To talk about our childhood?'

'I was just wondering where it all went wrong.' Nikolai looked out over the lake. 'It used to be you and me, remember? Betta tagging along, Giuliana furious when we said she was too young, Maria and the other castle kids following our lead. Days and days outside, escaping the confines of our castle, your tutor, our uncle and his lectures. Your mother aiding us with picnics and hidden treasure. It was idyllic, especially when your father was away and the Duke was too busy to worry about us. Idyllic, until one day you stopped playing and suddenly I was the enemy. I admit I hated you for it, partly because I lost my best friend and partly because you were so damn smug all the time. It was amusing shocking you, shocking my uncles, gaining and living up to a reputation. But when I spoke to Giuliana, I realised it was time to put a stop to all this.'

'Put a stop to what?' Tris could hardly believe what his cousin was saying. Was that how he saw it, their growing apart, growing up into such different men? One a playboy prince, partying in every continent, always in the tabloids and the gossip websites, the other dedicating himself to their country. He could hear their uncle, the Duke, reading out yet another headline in the cutting tone he reserved for Nikolai, impressing on Tris his duty to keep his cousin from the throne no matter what. And Tris had agreed. Nikolai was a womaniser, a spendthrift and a drunk and he had started early, embroiled in scandal long before he became an adult.

He looked over at his cousin, ready with a retort, but the words disappeared unsaid.

Nikolai had been married for five years now and Tris had heard no hint of infidelity. He was clearly a loving father and even if he hadn't settled to a job or role within the castle, he was no longer living in nightclubs and casinos.

Their uncle was convinced that Nikolai's marriage was a ploy simply to father a son and strengthen his own claim to the throne. Seeing the way he had held his daughter, Tris doubted it. Besides, Nikolai hadn't simply married; he had disappeared from the headlines. If his marriage was merely part of his game-playing, then wouldn't he have continued as before? Their laws demanded a wife and son but not fidelity. There was barely a king in their ancestral line who hadn't had a string of lovers throughout their reign.

Nikolai trailed a hand in the water; he suddenly looked very young and tired. 'I should have said something a long time ago but, I have to admit, it was too amusing being cast in the role of ne'er-do-well villain. But the truth is, Tris, I don't want to be the heir. I certainly don't want to be King.'

There was nothing but sincerity in his cousin's face. Tris folded his arms. 'Why now? What game are you playing, Nikolai?'

'Come on, Tris. I have the perfect life. I love my wife and my children, I have money, can travel anywhere I wish, have all the benefits of being a Ragrazzi and none of the negatives. Why would I want to change that to spend my life wrestling with Parliament and dealing with politics? Why would I want to have to put the country before my own desires? And, more importantly, having seen what being the heir did to you, why would I want to inflict that on my own son?'

They were all good points but, more importantly, sincerity rang in every word.

Nikolai straightened. 'I'd have told you this years ago, but you and the Duke were so convinced I was dying to step into your shoes, I thought I'd string you along for a little longer. But the truth is I am very happy to help you break the covenant. Make women equal in the line of succession, get rid of the ridiculous married-with-a-son-by-thirty-five rule, bring this beautiful and ridiculous country of ours up-to-date. We can ensure that me and mine move far away from the line of succession— let Elisabetta be your heir; she is probably the most qualified out of all of us.'

Tris stared out at the mountains across the lake, barely able to focus on the snow-topped peaks. Nikolai was offering him all he had ever wanted: an update to the succession laws, respite from a hasty marriage. But the freedom weighed heavily upon him.

'Why now?'

Nikolai didn't answer straight away, starting the engine up again and sending the boat flying through the lake. Looking back, Tris could see the villa receding, the guards' towers, hidden from the villa's view, clearly visible from here. They would have binoculars trained on them, their every move tracked. His freedom was, as ever, merely illusory.

Finally, Nikolai slowed the boat down again, running a hand through his hair, his expression thoughtful, his grey eyes sadder than Tris had ever seen them. 'I don't know why my father turned out so differently to his brothers,' Nikolai said. 'The Duke is as joyless and obsessed with tradition as your father was. If only my father had still been alive to be joint guardian after your father died, maybe he could have tempered the Duke's influence. But maybe it was already too late.' Nikolai's father had died in a plane crash when his son had been just fourteen. The tragedy should have brought the cousins closer together, but instead they had been pushed further apart. It was around that time that Nikolai had started to drink and party. Older and wiser now, Tris could see that grief had played its part in his cousin's rebellion. Back then he had merely censured him. No wonder Nikolai had called him smug. He deserved a far more stinging reproof than that.

'I couldn't believe it when I heard that he'd arranged a marriage for you, and that you simply went along with it,' Nikolai continued. 'When the rumours of your intended's disappearance started, I have to admit I was pleased. Not because that left you in an awkward situation, but because it gave you a chance of avoiding your father's mistake, marrying for prestige and position not for love. Marriage is a gift, Tris. My wife makes me a better man every day; you may not believe that but it's true. To marry because of a contract, to marry because of a ridiculous law put in place hundreds of years ago is wrong. If I really hated you, if I really was envious of you, maybe I'd let you carry on. But we were good friends once, practically brothers, and I can't help hoping that a good marriage, to someone who truly loves you, might help you remember the boy you used to be, not the man your father forced you to be.'

Nikolai stopped abruptly, red colouring his haughty high cheekbones. 'I can't believe I just said all that; blame my wife. She believes in talking about feelings. And she wanted me to come here today to tell you this. To set you free. Maybe it's too late for us to be friends again, Tristano, but we are family. It would be good to remember that more often.'

Tris didn't, couldn't, speak as Nikolai picked up speed once again, steering the boat round in a wide arc before heading back towards the jetty. Nikolai was going to help him change the inheritance laws, update them so his sister could be his heir, so that he could become King without a wife and a son beside him. Everything he had planned was now possible—without Amber. He didn't need her, not any more.

The thought echoed around and around in his mind. He no longer needed her, nor did he need the baby she carried. She was free. She could carry on with the life she had built for herself, the life she loved, surrounded by people who cared for her. She had chosen her own path, walked away from her title, fortune and royal destiny without so much as a backward glance. Now she could resume that path guilt-free. It was within his gift to give it to her.

His heart clenched, the pain so fierce, so all-encompassing he almost gasped aloud. It might be within his gift but he didn't *want* to set her free. He didn't want to wake up alone, didn't want to spend the rest of his life in his soulless, impersonal apartments, no time to work out who he was and what he wanted. He liked the way she teased him, enjoyed watching the way she put so much energy into educating him and the pleasure she got when he reported back that he liked a book or a film or a song she had chosen, how she tried to argue with him when he didn't.

He liked the way she was so wholehearted in everything she did, whether that was baking enough food for an entire children's party, filling an e-reader with a library's worth of books or explaining to him in vivid detail just why the original movie was the only one worth watching. Everything she did she did in luminous colour, such a contrast to his own grey life, and she lit up his soul.

His thoughts continued to whirl relentlessly on, examining his feelings in painful forensic detail. He liked the way she drew him out, was interested not just in what he was but in who he was, his title the least meaningful thing about him. The way she embraced everything they did, no matter how dull, how interested she was to meet new people, to discover new things. How she'd sat next to him on the balcony last night as once again he'd named the stars and she'd related the myth behind every constellation, making them laugh as she attempted to make sense of the shapes each constellation was meant to represent. She had an insatiable appetite for life and all it offered, those lonely years in her grandmother's penthouse watching rather than doing making nothing too small to interest her.

There were lots of things he liked about her. Most of all he liked how real he felt with her, but marriage was a two-way deal. What did he have to bring to the table except a title she didn't want and to be a hands-on father for her child? Their child.

Tris knew all too well that Amber's own sense of responsibility and a longing for family weighed heavily in his favour. But was that enough? He loved her, appreciated her efforts to make the relationship work, but he wasn't kidding himself. Amber was working hard because that was what she did. She made the best out of every situation.

Hang on…he *what*? His mind skidded back. He *loved* her?

Tris almost laughed aloud with the inevitability of the discovery. Of course he did. He'd been drawn to her the moment he first saw her, the dazzling bridesmaid with a glorious mane of hair and the wide smile. But he'd fallen in love with the gallant, open-hearted girl who still believed in love and kindness and hope even after her sad and difficult teenage years. Amber might admit to dreaming of rescue, but she'd buckled up and rescued herself. She had a courage and spirit that made her beautiful within as well as without. But he wasn't kidding himself; she was trying to forge a relationship with him because that was what she did, but she didn't love him. And she dreamed of love; she'd been frank about that from the beginning.

With a start, Tris realised the boat had slowed and they were back at the jetty, Nikolai looking at him quizzically, waiting for him to throw the rope around the mooring pole. Hurriedly, Tris gathered it in his hands and with practised ease looped it around the pole. He pulled the rope until the boat was tight against the jetty and the two men clambered out.

With a deep breath, Tris turned to his cousin. 'Thank you.' It was all he could manage, his head filled with too many thoughts and scenarios and feelings.

'I'm sorry things got to this stage,' Nikolai said. 'I'm fully aware how much I'm to blame, that I never reached out even after your father died. I hope it isn't too late.'

'Me too.' With a jolt of surprise, Tris realised he meant the words. 'It couldn't have been easy coming here today.'

'It wasn't. I had to bring my small daughter to give me courage; there was no way she'd allow me to turn back, not when I'd promised her that she'd see her cousins and she could paddle in the lake. But I had to come. My father used to say how vivid and alive your mother was when he first met her, but after several years married to your father she became just a shadow of herself. That all the expectation and your father's autocratic ways nearly crushed her. How he wished he had said or done something earlier. I didn't want to stand by and see history repeat itself. Maybe I'm wrong, maybe you and the Princess are meant to be, but either way I want you to go into marriage for the right reasons.'

'Come to the villa, Nikolai. Stay for dinner, you and Isabella. My sisters would like that, I'd like that.'

'Thank you.' Nikolai smiled, looking so like the carefree youth Tris remembered it was impossible not to smile back, despite the tumult of emotions tumbling around his brain. 'That would be good.'

The two men walked back to the villa side by side in a surprisingly companionable silence as Tris came to a resolution, as painful as it was necessary. Tonight he would play the host and enjoy the evening with his family and the woman he loved.

Tomorrow he would set her free.

CHAPTER FIFTEEN

'IT'S BEEN SO lovely to see you again.' Amber embraced Elisabetta with a warm hug. 'And absolutely gorgeous to meet you both.' She hugged first Talia and then Giuliana before stepping back, oddly bereft as the girls headed towards the car.

How ridiculous! Talk about an overreaction. She barely knew them for a start, and it wasn't as if they were going far. Elisabetta was returning to the castle, where she both lived and worked, Talia to the University of Elsornia which was based in the country's charming capital city just a few miles from the castle, whilst Giuliana needed to report back at the airbase just outside the city. She and Tris would be returning themselves in just a couple of days; she could renew her acquaintance with his sisters at any time. So why did this feel more like a *goodbye* than a *see you soon*?

As Tris walked his sisters back to their car, Amber tried to shake off the foreboding that had plagued her ever since Nikolai's unexpected arrival. She knew she was just being silly yet somehow her usual pep talks weren't helping and every hour her feeling that things weren't right deepened. She couldn't put her finger on why exactly. After all, Nikolai and Tris had returned from their boat trip if not the best of friends, cordial and with an understanding that evidently astonished Tris's sisters. Nikolai had even stayed until late the previous evening, before scooping up his adorable small daughter to drive her home, laughing that they would both be in trouble with his wife for staying out so late.

Sure, Tris had slept in his own room last night but that had been to allay any suspicions his sisters might have had about their relationship while it was still so fragile and undecided. But Amber had still half expected him to tiptoe down the corridors to her room after she had gone to bed and lain awake far too late waiting for him. She knew he was probably just being careful and had decided not to risk sneaking in, but it had been hard to sleep with his absence somehow filling the bed far more than his actual presence did.

She had also expected him to make an announcement about the baby, or maybe mention it casually while they were out walking, but nothing had been said. Elisabetta was obviously expecting him to say something too, judging by the quizzical glances she had sent Tris's way throughout the evening and today. Amber wanted to believe that Tris had decided to give her more time to decide, to ensure she wasn't ambushed by his excited sisters, but the explanation didn't quite ring true. His distance seemed emotional as well as physical, all the closeness and intimacy gone, as if he were now acting her suitor instead of becoming her lover.

Amber watched him as he closed the car door, standing back as Giuliana reversed the car and he waved his sisters goodbye. There was no discernible difference in him that she could articulate; he was still lighter and warmer than he had been back at the castle, but she *felt* a difference. The lightness seemed forced, his good humour put on, and she would look up to find him gazing at her with such a deep sadness in his eyes that her stomach twisted and her chest ached to see it.

She waved to the Princesses until the car disappeared behind the closing gates before turning to Tris as he made his way slowly towards her. They were alone once more. She should be looking forward to another comfortable evening together, enjoying the still so new intimacy whilst anticipating the night after their separation the night before; instead the silence was weighted with expectation and an air of something momentous left unsaid.

'Should we go inside?' Amber asked with as breezy a smile as she could manage Other words trembled on the tip of her tongue: what had Nikolai said? What was wrong? But the words stayed unsaid; she wasn't sure she wanted to hear the answer. Folding her hands into fists, she tried again but still couldn't speak. She wasn't usually a coward, preferring to make the most out of any situation, no matter how bleak it might seem. Her Pollyanna attitude had got her through tighter spots than this, and yet her usual courage ebbed away. Looking at Tris's set face, it was hard to feel anything but apprehensive.

'Go in? Yes, that seems best. Amber, there is something I need to say to you. Could you spare me five minutes?'

'Of course.' Her apprehension heightened, the cool civility in his voice chilling her. The politeness of his request was so at odds with the companionship they'd shared. Something had happened, something linked to Nikolai's unexpected arrival and their long trip out on the lake. Amber swallowed. She had thought she was used to being alone but not since her teens had she felt as isolated and friendless as she did right now.

Following Tris into the sitting room, Amber perched on a sofa, folding her hands neatly, feeling a little like she had as a teenager sitting in her grandmother's formal, overstuffed room, waiting to be told how to live her life. Sometimes she thought she'd never get rid of her grandmother's critical voice in her head, telling her she was too loud, too exuberant, too impulsive, too untidy. Not regal enough, not poised enough, not good enough.

Elisabetta had warned her that news of her reappearance was beginning to leak out. Amber knew that she couldn't avoid facing her past any longer; she needed to visit her grandmother, not to berate her or blame her but to lay all her ghosts to rest before the baby came.

The irony didn't escape her; if she took Tris with her she would merely be confirming to her grandmother that the harsh treatment and isolation had been right and had led to the desired outcome. Conversely, turning up as a single mother would probably have the same effect, proving that she couldn't be trusted to behave in an appropriate fashion on her own. But she no longer yearned for her grandmother's approval, no longer considered her family. Her opinion didn't matter. Any future relationship would be on Amber's terms, if they had one at all.

She also needed to take control of her own

fortune and look at how she could redistribute it, right the wrongs of her great-grandfather when he'd extracted the money from their small country. Tris was right; the best way would be through some kind of charitable foundation. It was that kind of forward thinking that made him such a good king. A good king and a good man.

She pushed the thoughts from her head and tried instead to concentrate on the scene unfolding before her, feeling more like a spectator than a participant. Tris hadn't joined her on the sofa; he stood in front of the window, his expression becoming bleaker and bleaker as he seemed to search for the right thing to say.

The silence stretched on until she could take it no longer. 'Tris, what's happened? Something's changed between yesterday and today; is it to do with Nikolai?'

Tris inhaled. 'Nikolai came here to tell me that he will support my bid to change the constitution.'

Okay. But that was good news, wasn't it? 'In what way? To make it possible for you to be King now, without a son? That's brilliant! It must be such a relief for you.' Numbness crept over her as she saw Tris wince at her hearty tone. But hiding behind good humour and positivity had been her defence for far too long; she couldn't drop it now.

'Exactly that. More, we have decided to legislate to ensure that the current generation will benefit from the change in the law. This means that the oldest child will inherit whenever the existing monarch dies or abdicates, regardless of age, marital status or offspring. By doing so, he has effectively removed himself from the succession as all three of my sisters now come before him. If Parliament ratifies these changes, and there is no reason for them not to with the current existing heirs both sponsoring the bill, I can be officially crowned within the year, with Elisabetta taking on the role as the formal heir to the throne. She will be eminently suited to the role.'

'Oh, yes, Elisabetta will be perfect,' Amber agreed, her hand creeping to her stomach. Surely Elisabetta would only be heir for a short while? If she and Tris were to marry then, no matter whether she was expecting a boy or girl, their baby would inherit the throne one day. Wasn't that what these changes meant?

Only…if Tris didn't have to get married, didn't have to have a son, then their marriage was no longer such a burning issue. In fact, it wasn't even necessary. Her chest tightened, the air closing in around her. No wonder he had withdrawn from her; she was no longer of any use to him.

Here was proof; the intimacy of the last week or so was merely an illusion. He'd tried hard, she had to give him that, but it had all been an act. Numbness began to steal over her as she tried to digest the implications. Had her instincts been so wrong? Was she so desperate after all for a happy-ever-after that she had fallen for a façade?

It had seemed so real. 'I see.'

Tris tried to smile, but there was no happiness or warmth in it. 'The good news for you is that there is no longer any need for you to make a life here. You can go back to your normal life, your agency and your friends. I know how much you hate the idea of living in a castle, being a queen, living the life I must lead. Now you don't have to.'

'No. I suppose I don't.'

'I've ordered you a car; it will be here shortly to take you to the airport. You can go home, Amber. Your kindness in coming in the first place will never be forgotten. I can't tell you how much I appreciate it. But there's no need for you to sacrifice your happiness any longer. You're free.'

Amber tried to find the right words, but for once she, who could usually chatter on to anyone about anything, was lost. What was wrong with her? She should be happy. Tris was right; this was exactly what she wanted made easy and guilt-free.

She had done the right thing in giving both him and Elsornia a chance but they both knew that living in the confined box of roy-alty wasn't what she really wanted. Yes, she was pregnant, and he was the father, but this was the twenty-first century; she had a home, a job she loved and friends who, even if they were far apart, would always support her. She could and would love and raise their baby alone. Far better to do so than to raise it in a loveless marriage where hope and willingness to try would be bound to end in disappointment and bitterness.

She lifted her head and met his gaze. 'That sounds very sensible. I'll go and pack now. Tris, I'm glad that everything has worked out for you. But I hope you know that I still would like you to be part of our baby's life. Every child needs a father if at all possible, and I think you are going to make a pretty remarkable one. I know your position makes it a little more complicated and I would rather not be the subject of any kind of media circus, but I'm sure if we're careful we can find a way for you to be as hands-on as possible. If that's what you want.'

Tris blinked and for a second Amber could have sworn she saw sorrow and disappointment cross his face. 'Thank you. I would very much like to be involved. I don't intend to marry, not now I don't have to. I'm not sure it would be fair on any woman to always be second best to my role. But I would like to be a father, to be involved.'

Somehow, Amber managed a smile, even though her chest was ever tighter and her heart pulsing with a pain she couldn't identify. 'You're only thirty, Tris. And you have such a huge capacity for love; don't close yourself off from all that, please. I'd better go and pack. I am happy for you, really I am. You've got what you wanted; that must be amazing.'

She got up from the sofa, walked over to him and kissed his cool cheek, feeling him tremble under her touch. For one wild moment she wanted him to seize her, to hold her, to pull her to him and kiss her properly and tell her he couldn't live without her. But instead he stood stock-still as she walked from the room, blinking hot, heavy tears from her eyes.

An hour later, Amber stood outside the villa, the car and driver waiting for her and her small amount of baggage, Tris next to her, still so remote and unreachable. This was what he wanted; surely he should be happy?

Surely *she* should be happy instead of feeling utterly bereft. Sick with disbelief and unexpected loss.

'Text when you're safely home,' Tris said, his words so ordinary they seemed utterly incongruous in the charged, unhappy atmosphere.

'Of course.' Amber took a step towards the car then stopped. 'I'll let you know the date of the next scan. Maybe there's a way you can come, if you have time? I'll have been home for almost two months by then so no one will be watching us; we might make it work. I'll send you the date.' She couldn't help thinking that if he wasn't involved now, then he would just get more and more remote until he was barely part of their lives at all. The thought of a future without him in it was too bleak to contemplate.

'If you'd like me to be there then of course I will be. I don't intend to just abandon you, Amber. I hope you know that.'

'I do.' But her words were more hope than an affirmation. Tris didn't know what unconditional love, what family was, didn't know he could be integral to someone's happiness. He was so likely to assume that she and the baby would be better off without him, to think he offered nothing of substance. By leaving, was she just proving that assumption true?

But he wanted her to leave. Had ordered the car before he had even told her of the change in his fortunes.

The driver put her few bags in the car and Amber didn't move, still not quite ready to say goodbye. Tris stood framed by the villa, the white paint gleaming gold and pink thanks to the setting sun. Her eyes burned. The time she'd spent here had been the happiest of her adult life. Somehow, the villa felt like home.

'Okay then.' Tris leaned forward and dropped a single chaste kiss on her cheek. 'Thank you again. For everything.'

'Read the books, okay? And finish the playlist and watch the films; let me know what you think. And keep baking! You're not too terrible.' She took a reluctant step towards the car, still hoping, but she didn't know for what.

This was what she wanted. Why on earth did she feel as if she was being wrenched from all she held dear?

'I will.' He stepped away, face shuttered, mouth set firm.

'Goodbye, Tris. Look after yourself.' Amber took another few steps to the waiting car, where the driver held a door open for her. Suddenly, impulsively, she turned around. 'Tris? Why did you agree to marry me all those years ago?'

She didn't know why, but somehow the question had been niggling away for weeks now, and suddenly it felt imperative to have an answer. Amber knew she was a fool but the teenager staring out of the turret window at the park below, hoping for someone to rescue her, who had spent far too many bored hours weaving elaborate daydreams about the man standing opposite her, still yearned to hear him say that she was worth something. That she had been more than a title and a convenience.

Tris looked away, but not before she saw the bleakness in his eyes. 'You looked lonely,' he said. 'And I understood loneliness. I guess I thought that together we could forge some kind of companionship. That what I could offer you here was better than what you had there. But that was then; you're not that girl any more. You have a career you love, friends who are more like a family, you're confident and beautiful and you bring sunshine everywhere you go. You are going to be an amazing mother. And you deserve more than what I can give you. So go, shine, raise our baby to see life the way you do. I'll take care of you both financially, I hope you know that, but you're free, Amber. Enjoy that freedom for both of us.'

She held his gaze and saw his grey eyes darken and for one long breathless moment Amber thought he might change his mind. Even though she missed her life and the dreams she'd had before Emilia's wedding, she had new dreams now, dreams she had barely known before today and certainly never articulated, but dreams centred around the man in front of her.

'Tris?' The hope swelling in her chest was

almost unbearable as their gazes locked and she allowed all the emotion inside her to show in her expression, in her eyes, in the hand she held out towards him. But all he did was lean over to place one light kiss on her cheek before walking away. He didn't look back once.

CHAPTER SIXTEEN

'*SIGNORINA?*' THE DRIVER indicated the open door with a smile. 'I am ready to go if you are?'

Amber stood, torn, her old life beckoning, the life she'd been contemplating receding into the distance. All she had to do was get into the car, let the driver take her to the airport and she could be home, tucked up in her own bed before midnight. Things would never be exactly the same; she knew that even with the money Tris could give her, a secure home in Chelsea and the agency ensuring she would always have a job, raising a child mostly alone would be difficult, but she never shied away from hard work and a family of her own was all she'd ever dreamed of. This wasn't the picture book two point four children and big golden dog and house in the country of her dreams, but it was real and it was hers. All she had to do was get in the car...

And yet she stood, anchored to the spot, replaying Tris's every word in her mind. He'd never said that he *didn't* want her, but he had said more than once that he was setting her free. Obviously, he thought he was doing the right thing. Hadn't she told him herself how much she loved her life, how little she wanted to change it? So why was she still standing here, unable to get in the car and return to it, guilt-free?

Amber looked around, at the villa, warmed by the setting sun, the lake tranquil behind, the mountains purple in the distance. Did she really want to leave this land of mountains and lakes and valleys? Did she really want to throw away the chance of calling Tris's sisters her family? And, most importantly of all, did she really want a life without Tris in it? She closed her eyes and saw him, gazing up at the stars, expression intent as he explained the constellations to her. Saw him poised, camera in hand, finding beauty in a commonplace scene and helping her to see the beauty as well. She saw him covered in flour, doing his best to follow her instructions, making her laugh as he did so. She saw him sprawled on the sofa with a careless grace, watching a film for the first time, showing every emotion like a small child rather than a jaded adult. She saw him that first night, the way he moved, the way he watched her, the way he touched her… And she remembered the nights here in the villa, sensual and tender and, yes, loving.

Amber swallowed, every nerve reacting to the memory of his sweet, skilled lovemaking. Sure, at times he could be closed off, but she of all people understood the reasons for that. Underneath the dignity he wore like armour, there was a man capable of more love and passion than she'd ever believed possible, eliciting love and passion in response.

Love. The word slammed into her and she gasped at the impact. Of course she loved him, this proud man who bore his responsibilities with dignity, this seductive man who had whirled her away in a dance and changed her life, this thoughtful man who listened to her and made her want to be a better person. She'd expected to recognise love straight away, to be floored by it, but she'd confused love with desire. If love was easy to recognise then there would be no need to kiss frogs... this bone-deep need and certainty was nothing she'd ever felt or even comprehended before.

Was she really going to get in the car and drive away from the one man she had ever loved? He wasn't the Prince she'd daydreamed about in her lonely teens, no perfect knight in shining armour riding to her rescue. That was okay; she didn't need to be rescued.

But maybe he did.

Tris strode towards the lake, needing something physical and hard and exhausting to do. Chopping down a tree maybe, or sawing logs. Anything to stop him thinking, to stop him turning back to the house to beg Amber not to go. He was doing the right thing, the noble thing, so where was the comforting sense of righteousness, of peace? Instead the pain inside was almost overwhelming as he kept re-playing the confused expression in Amber's eyes, kept hearing her call his name.

Hang on, that wasn't his imagination. Tris stopped and looked back, incredulous, as he saw Amber making her way towards him, hair tumbling around her face as she hurried along the path.

'Is something wrong?' Panic warred with hope.

She stopped and folded her arms. 'Yes, there is something wrong.'

Panic won out. 'Amber? Do you feel ill? The baby?'

'Not physically, but with this whole situation. You don't get to decide for me, Tris.'

'Amber...'

'When I was twelve my grandmother took me away from everything I knew and told me my entire life was flawed. She told me she knew how I should dress, what I should eat. Who I should be friends with, what I should do with my own time, and she was wrong. The only thing she might have been right about was who I should marry, but not for the right reasons.'

The air stilled around him, as if time had stopped and only the two of them existed. 'It's okay, Amber, there's no need for you to be here. Honestly.' No need but his own almost overwhelming need to hold her. Tris stood very still, watching her as she threw her hands up in frustration.

'You told me you are setting me free as if I'm some kind of bird you caged, but I'm not. I have my own mind, Tris, and I get to make it up. I am *always* free, no matter where I am, no matter what's happening because I don't let anybody cage me, not any more. If I decide to marry you it's because that's what I want, not because I've been coerced into some kind of sacrifice in order to do the right thing. Do you understand that?'

'I… What are you saying, Amber?'

'I'm saying you don't get to push me away before I get to tell you that I love you. You don't get to decide on your own that I don't need you. Because I do. I need you and I want you and I love you, Tris. I don't want you to hop in and out of this baby's life, but to be there all the time.'

Was this a dream? Was he hallucinating here on the lake shore while Amber was really on her way to the airport? She looked and sounded real, but the things she was saying made no sense. She couldn't really love him; this had to be her sacrificing herself, just the way he was trying to sacrifice his own happiness for her. It was almost funny in a twisted kind of way.

'I appreciate what you're saying, Amber, but...'

'You're not listening to me, Tris. I'm not making some kind of grand gesture, not being some kind of selfless martyr. I am, in fact, being very selfish indeed and claiming exactly what I want. I don't want to have to live without you, Tris, I don't want to go back to Chelsea alone. I want to stay here, marry you and raise a child together. Only...if that's what you want too. If you don't then please just say...' Her voice petered out and the fire in her eyes dimmed. Dimmed because of him, because he was just standing there like an utter fool.

'You really want to stay? With me?' He still couldn't believe it, even though sincerity rang true in every word, in every line of her body.

She smiled then, her whole face lit from within. 'You were my first crush, Tris, even though I pretty much made up your personality. To be honest, I wasn't really sure what I wanted, and my imaginings were a little dull. Lots of holding car doors open for me, bowing over my hand and staring in awe as I descended grand staircases in gorgeous ball gowns.'

'All the above could be arranged; just give me the word. We have plenty of grand staircases at the castle,' he promised, and she laughed.

'Maybe sometimes for old times' sake. Back then I fell in love with an ideal, a face I saw occasionally, and it was that ideal I wanted to sleep with at the wedding. A way of finally putting the past behind me. But you're not that fantasy figure; you're so much better than that. So much more. I know you hide it, even from yourself, but you've shown yourself to me and what I see is pretty damn special. I see a man who is kind and considerate and clever, who can describe the stars to me and makes me want to listen all night. A man who is far too sexy for his own good, a man who will do anything for the people he loves. A man I trust with my heart because I know he'll always look after it. Tris, you are right, this isn't the life I wanted, but if it's a life I share with you, then it's the life I choose. If you will have me.' Doubt crept into her voice and tore at Tris's heart.

He tilted her chin and smiled into her eyes. 'If I'll have you? Amber Blakeley, there is nothing I want more. I can't claim to have fallen in love with you back in New York; you were just a child. But I did see you then, I noticed you and I wanted to help you. I didn't fall in love with the bridesmaid either, although I thought she was one of the most special, most beautiful people I'd ever met. I fell in love with you, the you right here with all your enthusiasms and optimism and dreams. I want your light in my life.'

'Always,' she whispered, her green eyes filled with tears and he wiped them away tenderly.

'I love you, Amber, not because you carry our child and not because I need a queen, but because of everything that you are. Will you marry me, despite all that comes with me? I know we haven't known each other that long, and if things were different then I would have loved to have courted you properly…'

Amber reached up to lay a hand on his cheek. 'But things are the way they are. Fun as courting sounds, I know it's easier if we marry before the baby is born, but there's no reason you can't court me after we're married.'

'Every day,' he vowed, and she smiled softly into his eyes.

'I want to marry you sooner rather than later and embrace all that comes with you, because that's what makes you who you are. I love you, Tris, and I can't wait for the baby to be here and for us to be a family, just like I always dreamed. Here, in the castle or anywhere as long as we are together that's all that matters. Life has taught me that.'

'I love you too, and I promise to do everything in my power to make you happy every day,' Tris vowed as he finally kissed her the way he'd always wanted to, with all the love and hope and passion bursting within him, her own kiss warm and sweet and passionate. As he held her, Tris promised himself that she would never be lonely again; like all the best fairy tales he might have rescued her, but she'd turned around and rescued him right back. And that was how all the best happy-ever-afters were supposed to be.

EPILOGUE

'Oh, Emilia, he is *gorgeous*.' Harriet picked up the three-week-old heir to the Armarian throne and cradled him tenderly. 'You clever, clever girl.' She looked over at Amber and grinned. 'Wouldn't it be amazing if your Rosa and Emilia's Max made a match of it?'

'No royal matchmaking betrothals in our households, thank you very much,' Amber retorted as she adjusted the frills on Rosa's christening gown—Tris had made several inroads in updating some of Elsornia's more antiquated laws over the last year, but even he couldn't save their daughter from being baptised in the traditional Elsornian royal christening gown, a delicate Victorian confection comprising of several long layers of silk and lace and more buttons than any baby should have to endure. 'Just because mine worked out in the end doesn't mean we're reviving that particular custom. But if I was a matchmaking mama, then obviously I would choose Max to be my son-in-law. Em, he is beautiful. And you look amazing, Thank you for coming so soon after the birth.'

'I wouldn't miss my goddaughter's christening for the world.' Emilia reached out to stroke three-month-old Rosa's cheek. 'I'm so excited to celebrate with you, little one.'

'How are you feeling, Amber?' Alex asked from the sofa she was sharing with her two soon-to-be nieces, a beautiful vintage diamond ring glinting on her left hand. 'It was so brave of you to invite your grandmother. Brave and very forgiving. I'm not sure I could have been so generous.'

Amber looked round at her friends, her heart so full of love and happiness she could hardly believe it. Although they still owned the Happy Ever After Agency, both Emilia and she had had to take a step back, thanks to their royal duties, and since her marriage Harriet spent more and more time in Brazil with Deangelo. The Chelsea house was still the agency's headquarters, but paid staff occupied the vintage desks, the bedrooms turned into more offices for the increasing number of employees whilst Alex ran the agency from the countryside home she shared with Finn and his nieces. Amber spoke to at least one of her friends every day, but they hadn't all been in the same room since Harriet's wedding eight months before. To have the four of them here, in her charming sitting room overlooking the palace gardens, celebrating her daughter's birth, was very special indeed. Even her grandmother's presence in the castle couldn't disrupt her happiness.

Gently shifting her sleeping daughter to her other arm, Amber smiled at Alex, who was as elegant as ever in a green silk shift dress. 'When I visited my grandmother in New York she wasn't the fierce autocrat I remembered; she was just a lonely woman. All she had were her dreams of a throne in a country that doesn't exist any more, acquaintances instead of real friends, no hobbies, no one or anything to love. It made me feel so sorry for her. I have so much and she so little—inviting her to the wedding and the christening was the least I can do. We'll never have the kind of relationship I used to yearn for, but that's okay. I have Tris, Rosa and his sisters, and I have you three, my sisters in every way that counts.'

'You'll always have us,' Emilia said softly, her words echoed by Harriet and Alex.

'And you me. Our lives have changed so much in the last two years, but we're still the same girls who dreamed of our own business and made it happen, the same girls who met one Christmas Eve and realised we weren't alone. Marriage and babies don't change that; it just enhances it, makes our family even bigger. Rosa is so lucky to have you three as her godmothers and aunts, just as I am lucky to have you as friends and sisters.'

She blinked, emotional tears threatening to spill down her cheeks, relieved when the door opened to reveal Tris, smart in his dress uniform, flanked by Deangelo, Finn and Laurent, who immediately made a beeline for his son, pride etched on his features.

'The cars are here,' Tris said, carefully lifting Rosa off Amber's knee and then extending a hand to help her rise. Amber curled her fingers around his, grateful for his strength and solicitude. 'Ready to get this young lady christened?'

'Absolutely.' Amber watched her friends file from the room: Deangelo and Harriet, hand in hand, Finn and Alex, shepherding his nieces in front of them, sharing an intimate smile as they did so, Laurent and Emilia, his arm around her as she carried their newborn son. She turned to press a kiss on Tris's cheek. 'I love you,' she whispered. 'Thank you for making me so very happy.'

'I should be the one thanking you,' Tris said, his eyes soft as he smiled down at their daughter. 'For everything you do and everything you are.' He squeezed her hand. 'Come on, let's celebrate our daughter with our friends and family. She's done the impossible; my mother is considering getting a house in the city so she can see Rosa regularly and your grandmother is both here and behaving. She's a miracle child.'

'She is.' Amber allowed Tris to escort them

from the room, knowing she would be able to face the pomp and ceremony of a royal christening with him by her side, flanked by her friends. They'd named the agency well all those months ago. Life was bound to have bumps in the road, its trials and tribulations, but as long as they kept loving each other then she knew they would live happily ever after, just as she'd always dreamed.

* * * * *

LET'S TALK

Romance

For exclusive extracts, competitions
and special offers, find us online:

- **f** facebook.com/millsandboon
- **◎** @millsandboonuk
- **▼** @millsandboon

Or get in touch on 0844 844 1351*

For all the latest titles coming soon,
visit millsandboon.co.uk/nextmonth

*Calls cost 7p per minute plus your phone company's price per
minute access charge

Want even more
ROMANCE?

Join our bookclub today!